BODY
OF
KNOWLEDGE

BRYCE W. ANDERSON

BODY OF KNOWLEDGE

PUBLISHED BY BRYCE W. ANDERSON

COPYRIGHT © 2008 BY BRYCE W. ANDERSON

ISBN: 978-0-6152-1855-7

PRINTED IN THE UNITED STATES OF AMERICA

STOP.
TAKE A LOOK AS YOU PASS BY.
AS YOU ARE NOW, ONCE WAS I.
AS I AM NOW, YOU SOON WILL BE.
SO PREPARE YOURSELF FOR ETERNITY.

-EPITAPH ON CLINTON BRONSON'S GRAVE (1909 · 1985)

FOREWORD

An ant has two stomachs. I know this because my neighbor told me; and to my knowledge he never lied to me. As a matter of fact, ants were the only things he could talk about when I first met him. It seems such a long time that I knew him; but it was only two months. Two very short months. It's fascinating how a person's attitude and feelings about someone, or for that matter, about life in general, can change so much in such a short time.

Two months ago I hardly knew the meaning of the word 'time'. Another thing I learned from him: how to view everything from varying objective perspectives; especially with respect to time. If I had it to do over again, I'd have been more inquisitive. My wife Gwen accuses me of asking too many questions, but with him, I couldn't have asked enough. He knew everything. Is it possible to ask someone who knows everything too many questions?

But I did ask a lot of questions, and there were always answers. And I liked the answers. They fit. They were logical. They placed everything in perspective and made me see the picture as a whole.

I thought you might find it interesting why I thought the only logical thing I could do was kill him.

INTRODUCTION

During my junior year at the University of Montana, I was required to take a class taught by Dr. Ronald Wilson entitled CS 381 – Logic. We spent the majority of the semester discussing truth tables. The following is a very concise description of what a truth table is.

Let's start with the English sentence "I am a man." This simple sentence can have one of two values: either true, (represented by a 'T') or false (represented by an 'F'). If we assign the variable 'M' to the sentence "I am a man", the truth table of our statement would look like this:

M
F
T

The meaning of this truth table can be interpreted like this:

M (I am a man)
FALSE (I am not a man (I am a woman))
TRUE (I am a man)

Now let's add another variable 'G' and assign it to the simple sentence 'I wear glasses'. The truth table for the statement 'I wear glasses' would also have two solutions and be represented by the following truth table:

G (I wear glasses)
FALSE (I do not wear glasses)
TRUE (I wear glasses)

Interesting things begin to happen when you combine the two statements with conjunctions (the English words 'AND' and 'OR'). Let's combine our sentence 'M' (I am a man) using the 'OR' conjunction with our sentence 'G' (I wear glasses). In English, we have the following sentence: 'I am a man or I wear glasses.' The following would represent the truth table for all possible solutions of this sentence:

I am a man	OR	I wear glasses	Validity of the entire sentence (The Solution)
FALSE	OR	FALSE	FALSE (I am a woman and don't wear glasses)
FALSE	OR	TRUE	TRUE (I am a woman and wear glasses)
TRUE	OR	FALSE	TRUE (I am a man and don't wear glasses)
TRUE	OR	TRUE	TRUE (I am a man and I wear glasses)

Note that when using the 'OR' conjunction, when either of our two statements ('M' or 'G') is true the entire sentence is true. Let's compare this to the truth table of the 'AND' conjunction:

I am a man	AND	I wear glasses	Validity of the entire sentence (The Solution)
FALSE	AND	FALSE	FALSE (I am a woman and don't wear glasses)
FALSE	AND	TRUE	FALSE (I am a woman and wear glasses)
TRUE	AND	FALSE	FALSE (I am a man and don't wear glasses)
TRUE	AND	TRUE	TRUE (I am a man and I wear glasses)

With the 'AND' truth table, all elements of the sentence must be true for the entire sentence to be true. As opposed to the 'OR' truth table, which had three true conditions, there can be only one condition that will validate the entire sentence in an 'AND' truth table.

Truth tables can get quite messy, especially when you begin combining 'AND's', 'OR's', and 'NOT's' all in the same table. Suffice it to say that I have presented you with the most simple of truth tables here.

An interesting thing to note: the English word 'OR' is generally understood to be equated with the logical term 'EXCLUSIVE OR'. 'EXCLUSIVE OR' means it must be one or the other, but it cannot be both. To demonstrate this, let's examine a sentence you might tell your child after he or she has eaten all of their dinner:

"You can have cookies or cake for dessert."

Even your child understands this sentence to mean:

"You can have cookies or cake for dessert, but you can't have both."

These two sentences are entirely different things. Here is a side-by-side truth table for comparison (XOR = 'EXCLUSIVE OR'):

Cookies	**OR**	Cake	Solution		Cookies	**XOR**	Cake	Solution
FALSE	OR	FALSE	FALSE		FALSE	XOR	FALSE	FALSE
FALSE	OR	TRUE	TRUE		FALSE	XOR	TRUE	TRUE
TRUE	OR	FALSE	TRUE		TRUE	XOR	FALSE	TRUE
TRUE	OR	TRUE	TRUE*		TRUE	XOR	TRUE	FALSE*

The asterisked items are the only difference between the two tables, but because of them, the whole English language can be misunderstood if the differentiation between the two isn't made. This concept fascinates me, which may shed some light on why I became a computer programmer in the first place.

But it doesn't stop there. Truth tables describe the way I think. With practice, any statement can be made into a truth table and validated (or refuted) in your head.

Not only are truth tables applicable to computer science and English, but they have application in electronics as well. ('T' or 'F' can very easily be substituted with a '1' or a '0' – indicating 'on' or 'off'. I have actually designed a working model of a digital clock on a computer using nothing but truth tables.)

Now that you know a portion of how I think, maybe you'll understand me better as I try to unfold a story to you that I believe defies logic. Please keep in mind that what I might express in three or four pages is actually the culmination of a lifetime of thought. I wouldn't expect you to absorb, or adopt, any or all of my expressed thoughts, in one sitting; just as some of you may have to study the preceding diagrams several times to even begin to understand how truth tables operate.

The concepts presented in this book are, wherever possible, and to the best of my knowledge, based on fact. There were portions where researched historical data seemed to conflict with itself. In such instances, I either incorporated both, to the best of my ability, or used the most logical of the conflicting possibilities.

We are all gifted with a brain and the power of reason. Ultimately, it is up to us what we decide to accumulate in our own Body of Knowledge.

1.
[UN]SETTLING IN

"The meeting of two personalities is like the contact of two chemical substances: if there is any reaction, both are transformed."
                                    - Carl Jung (1875 – 1961)

It started one Friday afternoon in the early summer of 1991. I gazed out my front window at the home across the street that had stood there vacant for over five months. When it was occupied, it blended well with all the other ranch-style houses on the block. But since the former occupants had left, the lawn had gone to seed and it looked very much like what it was; a vacant home. I kept reminding myself to get over and clean up the yard so I wouldn't have to look at it; but that wasn't going to happen and I knew it: I'm too lazy.

Today the house looked different, though; instead of a vacant lot with a 'For Sale' sign poking up through the three-foot tall weeds, a U-Haul trailer sat jackknifed in the driveway, angled toward the front door. It was the tiniest U-Haul I'd ever seen, and I wondered how anyone who could afford to buy that house could pack all their belongings into such a small space.

Normally, I would have ducked down under the window and slithered to the back of the house so as not to be seen, and thereby suckered into lending a hand, but what I was witnessing kept me captivated. First of all, the man was wearing clothes I hadn't seen since the last time I browsed the clearance rack at the local Goodwill store. Secondly, he was squatting down on his haunches like he was trying to control a terrible bowel ache. He just squatted there, staring at the driveway beneath him, not moving a muscle. Because he faced the other direction, I made the decision to stay and view the outcome, expecting him to bolt for the bathroom at any moment. That didn't happen. I must have stood there for a full two minutes; and he didn't move once. There was definitely something wrong with this guy.

I shook my head as I made my way to the front door, knowing that I was being duped into helping this Bozo lug a three-ton refrigerator up a flight of stairs, but it didn't seem to make any difference to me at the time. I needed to see what was going on with this guy who could squat and stare at the sidewalk without moving for a whole three minutes.

I made a quick glance up and down the cul-de-sac to see if someone was out mowing their lawn or working on their car, but it was still fairly early in the afternoon, and there was no one in sight. I was going to have to fly solo on this mission.

As I made my way across the street I kept expecting him to glance in my direction with a look of complete confidence on his face that suggested 'Gotcha'. As I made my final approach, I craned my neck to the side as if he might jump up at any moment and slash my throat. That didn't happen either. Instead, I cleared my throat and muttered, "You need a hand with something?"

Without so much as looking up or even acknowledging my existence, almost as if he had known me for years, he said, to no one in particular, "Did you know an ant has two stomachs?"

"I beg your pardon?" I replied, assuming that I was having problems with my hearing.

"An ant has two stomachs," he said. "It has a smaller one in the front of his abdomen, called a crop, and the larger, real stomach, attached behind it. When a friend brushes the ant's mandible with its antenna, the ant regurgitates honey into the mouth of its friend. That way ants can store food for sharing, while at the same time digesting the food they need to survive."

"Fascinating," I replied, half interested, half wondering who the nut we had moving in across the street from us was.

"Some worker ants become so engorged with food that they literally can't move. They just lay there like a slug until enough friends come by so as to remove the contents of his crop until he can move again," he continued, indifferent to my indifference. "It's kind of like a nature-built refrigerator."

There it was. The refrigerator line, I knew he'd get to it, just not this fast. This guy was sly. Go ahead, I thought, break it to me; I was dumb enough to fall for this stupid trick. I might as well blow the rest of my Friday evening helping this lunatic set up camp in my neighborhood; no other psychotics on the block I can lend a hand to this evening.

"Bryce Anderson," I said, extending my hand, while at the same time hoping he'd at least glance up at me from the single red ant that he'd spent upwards of four minutes watching now.

"I beg your pardon," he responded warmly as he arose. "JP. It's nice to meet you."

"JP?" I pondered out loud. "Is that short for anything?"

"Not as far as you know," he quipped while fumbling with the latch on his U-Haul.

He may not have been divulging much, but it was crystal clear he was hiding something. He had intended to be humorous with his last remark, but it was obvious he'd used it before, and I was not going to be able to pry any more information from him. So I didn't try; I left it at that, which disturbed me greatly. Unanswered questions and I don't get along well at all.

"I don't have much in here," he said. "And I don't want to tie up your whole afternoon. If you'd just give me a hand with my couch, I'd greatly appreciate it."

As he swung the back doors open, I gasped in disbelief. The U-Haul was indeed small, but his belongings only filled half the space. A couch that looked like it may have been popular in the early seventies absorbed the bulk of the space. It had a puke green background color with wild orange and purple flowers plastered on it. A yellow dot adorned the center of each colored flower. Aside from his psychedelic couch, he had a small black and white television set, and some pillows and blankets. All I could see other than that were books; thousands of them. They weren't even packed in boxes. They were just placed neatly on the couch and floor. He must have driven incredibly slowly to get here so that they didn't sprawl all over the place.

"So what brings you to Montana?" I asked.

"The land. The people. I heard it's a great place to live. I came to see if it was true."

"Where you from?" I asked.

"I came by way of Colorado Springs," he offered, reluctantly.

I wondered if that meant that he actually lived in Colorado Springs, or if he drove through Colorado Springs on his way from Detroit. Either way, I decided not to pursue it. I remained silent for a while. I waited at the back of the trailer while he climbed up and over the couch to the front to grab the far end of it. He carefully lowered the books that were on the couch to the floor of the trailer. We hefted it quite easily and ascended the four stairs to his porch. We set it down as he unlocked the front door.

"Let's just set it right here in the front room," he nodded toward the far wall.

We plodded back to the trailer and I hefted some rather large books into my arms to help him with the payload. As I picked up the books, I noted that they all seemed to be extremely old, although each one of them was in excellent condition. "I'll go over to my house and get some boxes to make these easier to carry in, if you'd like," I chimed.

"That's really not necessary," he remarked, as he removed the books from my arms. "You've really given me all the help I need, already. Thanks for lending a hand," he turned from me and ascended the stairs again.

I glared at him for a moment wondering whether or not I should protest, but it was obvious to me that he didn't want any more help, whether he needed it or not. Something was up with this guy, and it wasn't natural.

I sauntered across the street and opened our front door when I was struck by a thought. I turned briskly and stared at the front of the old green box-like jalopy that had pulled the tiny trailer to our neck of the woods. As I suspected: his car brandished current Florida plate number PKA 37Y; not Colorado plates, as he had led me to believe.

Partially relieved for having salvaged my afternoon, but very concerned over who, or what, had just moved in across the street, I made my way through the door and into the kitchen to hunt for something cold to drink. I needed to do some detective work.

2.
THE INTERNET SEARCH

"The important thing is not to stop questioning.
Curiosity has its own reason for existing."
- Albert Einstein (1879 – 1955)

As a computer programmer, I thought I was familiar with *what* the Internet had to offer, but I wasn't prepared for *how much* it had to offer. I immediately found that simply by entering the keywords FLORIDA CRIMINAL RECORD in the search box on my Excite home page that I had 74 sites at my disposal that offered me a wide variety of reports about pretty much any criminal I wanted. Most were for the rock-bottom price of $24.95. I scanned pages for half an hour until I came across a site that had precisely what I was looking for:
http://www.dc.state.fl.us/activeinmates/search.asp.

I found it useful because it scanned every available database and you only needed to put in what you knew about the guy. That was helpful to me because I had a basic description of the guy, but I was fairly certain his name wasn't JP. I did, however, put in JP as the last name and clicked the little 'search aliases' box underneath it.

    Race: White
    Sex: Male
    Eye Color: Brown
    Hair Color: Black
    Height Range: From 5'7" to 6'0 (He was shorter than me, and I'm six feet)
    Weight Range: From 160 lbs to 190 lbs
    Age Range: From 35 yrs To 55 yrs (How old was this guy? – hard to tell)

Offence Category: All
County of Commitment: All
Current Location: All
Show Photos: Yes

And there it was; what I was sure would unveil the animal that had just become my neighbor. I popped the SUBMIT REQUEST button at the bottom of the page. I waited impatiently for the results of my request.

Four matches: James P. Maddox, Jose Perez, John H. Pierce, and James B. Pleas. I took a second hard look at John Pierce, because he was almost bald, and hair can disguise a lot, but after a second view I determined there was no match there.

So I took out the 'JP' as the last name / alias and tried again. 591 hits, and I guarantee you I looked through every last one of them. He was not one of them. This was hopeless. I needed someone who knew what they were doing – definitely not me.

That's when I decided to give my friend Shane Faust a call. Shane worked for the Missoula County Sheriff's Office for about 30 years before he retired. He was actually my brother's friend's Dad, but I figured I was a close enough relation that he'd be more than willing to do me a favor on a Friday afternoon, nice day. Yeah, he'd be more than happy to help.

It took a substantial amount of coaxing, and having to endure several explanations that what I was asking him to do was both unethical and illegal, but he said he'd make a call to the dispatcher and see if she could run the plate through as a favor to him. I assured him that all I wanted to know was his real name, where he was from, and if he had a criminal record or not.

The rest of the evening came and went, and I was beginning to suspect I'd been blown off, but at long last the phone rang about 8:30. I picked it up on the second ring.

"Bryce, this is Shane."

"Yeah, thanks for getting back to me. It means a lot."

"Well, we ran the plates through, and they're legitimate. Florida PKA 37Y registered March of this year to a light green 1969 AMC Rambler. Registered to a man by the legal name of JP. His address at the time of registration was 5915 Grapevine Drive, Colorado Springs, Colorado, 80918. He has no criminal record whatsoever. Matter-of-fact, he didn't have much of a record at all. How old is this guy?"

"I'd say about 40, but I'm guessing," I said.

"Well, he's as clean as a guy can get. You're the proud owner of a new neighbor," he drawled.

There was a deafening pause for a moment as I heard him shuffle some papers. "You say this guy is about 40?" he questioned again.

"Probably between 35 and 45," I said.

"Hmmm, that's kinda strange," he said. "Marla gave me the whole scoop on this guy and I wrote down the stuff that I thought you might be interested in. There were two things that stuck out. The first was his date of birth. It was written on file as June 12, 13. I even asked her to verify the year to make sure it didn't say '73; and she assured me it was a 13 – as in 'thirteen stripes on the American flag'. She said it didn't even have an apostrophe. Now, unless the guy's an apparition that's not going to appear for another twenty-two years, that makes him 78 years old. I've never seen a 78 year old man that could pass for 40."

"Maybe that got screwed up when he changed his name to JP," I suggested.

"These are legal and lawful documents we're dealing with here, Bryce. Making screw-ups like that, especially two of them on the same page, is pretty close to being unheard of. Besides, there were no legal documents indicating he'd ever had a name change. As far as our records show, he's always been just 'JP'."

"You mentioned two things," I said. "What was the other thing?"

"Well," he stammered, "generally birth certificates are notarized at the bottom of the certificate within one to three days from the actual date of birth. This particular certificate was dated significantly later than that."

"How significant?" I retorted.

"The notarized date on this document was December 4, 1945."

"What does that mean?" I shrugged.

"It means your friend is either a really poor forger, or he has some friends in very high places."

"Why's that?" I questioned again.

"Well, creating a birth certificate 32 years after the actual date of birth isn't exactly an everyday event. The only time I've seen anything like this is under the witness protection program; when someone assumes a completely new identity, but even then there's no reason to alter the date of birth."

I had millions of things flying through my mind but I couldn't think of anything else to ask him. "I appreciate your time, Shane. I've been worrying about this guy since I first saw him and I'll sleep a little better tonight knowing he's clean." (Or at least smart enough to find ways to get around the system, I thought to myself.) "I'll keep this under my hat so you won't get in trouble."

"I don't blame you for being concerned, but it doesn't look like you've got anything to be worried about," he said. "I'm glad I could help. Tell your brother 'hi' for me."

"I'll do that. Take care, Shane, and thanks again."

So there it was. The cards were on the table and no one had won. I had more questions after I hung up the phone than I did before the call - not the least of which was a mental note to myself to ask my new 78 year-old neighbor, who could pass for being 40, where he worked out, and what his diet consisted of.

3.
BUYING THE FARM

"Oh, the good times when we were so unhappy."
- Alexander Dumas (1802 – 1870)

The day was almost gone, and I hadn't done a thing that I'd planned to do. Weekends are like that for me. I look forward to them all week, and when they finally hit, I'm either too tired, or the weather is too bad, to do anything I want to do. I wind up sitting on my butt until I'm aroused out of my stupor by the buzzer at 6:45 a.m. Monday morning: time to start all over again.

I did, however, have time to run to Wal-Mart and get the shampoo and aluminum foil that my wife Gwen had asked me to get yesterday, but I had forgotten.

I don't get to spend much time with my kids, so I asked them if they wanted to join me. Generally, three sets of glazed blue eyes glance up from their video games just long enough to grunt "No, thanks." But, lo and behold, tonight I was three for three. It must have been a painfully slow weekend for them, actually wanting to spend time with their Dad.

I was the first in the car. I watched in the rear-view mirror as two blonde girls, one little, one larger, buckled themselves in. The third little person, a dusty brunette, always brought up the rear. My son has a knack of always being the last one in the car, no matter where we're going. It's one of those little things you try to correct as a parent, but eventually concede the fact that it will never change. Tonight it didn't bug me so much, though. At least they were volunteering some of their quality Nintendo time to spend with their old man. Beggars can't be choosers.

We decided to play the 'T' or 'P' game on the way. I get 'P' and they get 'T', but it's three against one, so it evens the odds a bit. All Missoula license plates start with a '4T' or a '4P' – '4T' indicating a Missoula truck, '4P' indicating a Missoula passenger vehicle. Whoever counts the most plates of their type wins. Depending on which route I take, I can generally determine the outcome before the game ever starts. I like losing because it gives me an excuse to buy them an ice cream cone. It's uncanny how close the games have been, though.

It was approaching twilight, and I chose to take the most direct route down 39th, knowing full well that if I took the residential routes I'd certainly win, unless I drove with my eyes shut. The kids hate it when I do that, though. I believe the score was about 47 to 68 when my eyes caught hold of a Florida plate coming in our direction. I glanced up just in time to see the mystery man gliding by at what I considered to be a snail's pace. He certainly *drove* like a 78 year old man. Maybe that explains why none of the books in his trailer were askew.

I had gotten him out of my mind for all of about 5 minutes. Now he'd popped back in again.

"How many points did I have?" I asked.

"26!" my son quipped amidst a chorus of snickers from my daughters.

"Cheaters," I smiled back at them via the rear-view mirror.

After I'd picked up the shampoo, the aluminum foil, and eight 4-for-a-dollar candy bars that the kids talked me into, we made our traditional walk to the toys aisle. As my daughters browsed the Barbie's and my son sprinted to the dragons and swords, something caught my eye. There, on the shelf, as large as life, was an Original Uncle Milton's Ant Farm. I thought they had stopped making these things thirty years ago. According to the label, this "Best Classic

Toy Award" winning wonder included four connecting ant ports, tunneling sand, an antway traveling tube, an ant-watcher's manual, and a certificate to send to Uncle Milton himself for the complimentary ants.

To summarize, it was two transparent plastic panes held together by a frame of green plastic, with just enough space separating the windows to dump some ants in. These things were big fun in the fifties, or so I'd heard.

Twelve bucks. That's all it would take to reunite me with my misunderstood neighbor. It was a steal; I would have paid twenty for it. I threw it in the cart with the other stuff. Boy, was I excited. This is exactly what I was looking for. Tomorrow I would present the finest housewarming gift that could possibly be given. I could just see the tears flowing from JP's eyes as he reverently accepted my wondrous gift.

As it turned out, that's exactly what happened.

4.
MINOR COMPUTATIONS

"Not everything that counts can be counted,
and not everything that can be counted counts."
                                    - Albert Einstein (1879 – 1955)

Saturday morning has always started early for me. I perpetually make up my mind that I will sleep until noon, but it never happens. The sun ricochets off the pulled blinds and always seems to find its way to my eyes. I'm helpless, there's nothing I can do but get out of bed. Generally speaking, it's usually around 6:30 a.m. This morning, however, things were different. Because of the events that transpired yesterday, I was as giddy as a schoolgirl. I felt like a Father getting up just before the crack of dawn on Christmas day so he could see his kids race to see what Santa had brought them the night before.

After rolling out of bed and relieving myself of last night's build-up, I sauntered in to the kitchen and poured myself a bowl of raisin bran and unfolded the paper. Boris Yeltsin is inaugurated as the first freely elected president of the Russian Republic, what else is new? Nothing; this was boring, and I was anxious to get to the good stuff. With it being only 6:30 though, I couldn't exactly mow the lawn, I do have some degree of respect for my neighbors, who manage to sleep somewhat later than I do – although that sentiment is generally not reciprocated by their children who ride around on motor-scooters, that are forever stuck in first gear, 'til the wee hours of the morning.

I looked at the Ant Farm over on the cabinet. A smile must have appeared on my face as I wondered whether or not my new neighbor would actually use this thing, or if it was just an exercise in futility. Should I wrap it? That didn't seem to make much sense, but it did need sprucing up, so I looked through the garbage bag full of bows we keep in our closet and picked out a nice green one to perk up the looks of the gift. The shade of green blended with the box beautifully; and it didn't seem overdone, so I left it at that.

Now what? 6:35 and I can't mow the lawn. The kids are still asleep so I can't very well make them an omelet like I usually do on Saturday mornings. I wonder if my new neighbor gets up as early as I do.

I went to our front window and looked out across the street at what I thought would be an uneventful sight. To my elation, JP was bellying up to his front window, trying to hang drapes. Without further ado, I silently sprinted to my room, yanked on some old gray sweatpants and my blood donor T-shirt that I had inherited for being leeched, and made my way back to the front door without so much as pulling on a pair of shoes. Halfway across the street I realized I'd forgotten to bring along the reason for my neighborly visit. I bolted back to the kitchen and grabbed the present, this time slowing only slightly enough to throw on a pair of sandals. Now I was fully prepared.

As I hiked the steps of his front porch, I saw that he was no longer trying to hang drapes; and the drapes were not even visible. With my luck, they were probably lying in a heap under the window, and he'd forsaken the event to try and sleep again. Because I thought he might have gone back to sleep, I knocked on the door very lightly. As I was turning away, the door opened gently and there he was, dawned in a pair of Levis and a gray pullover sweatshirt. He stood with his right arm bent at the elbow and resting on his stomach, just above his navel. It reminded me of paintings I had seen of Napoleon Bonaparte, with his hand tucked under his coat.

"Good morning," he said very cheerily, as though he'd been waiting for me. "Come on in."

I sauntered in and took a quick note of the surroundings. A musty smell hung in the air, which was to be expected. Five months of vacancy is a long time for a house to remain smelling 'April-fresh'. The front room was comfortably large, with a fireplace at the far end. The lone green couch stuck out like a sore thumb against the bare pale walls of the room. Kitty corner from where I stood was a doorway, leading to what appeared to be the kitchen. Off to my right, a hallway led to four doors that were all partially open; one of which must have been a bathroom.

After I'd taken in the scene, I said, "I saw you about to plunge through your front window and thought you could use a hand."

"That I could," he replied. And then added, "You're up early," as he made his way to the kitchen. "Can I get you some orange juice?"

"Sure," I replied, wondering what he kept it in, since I was fairly sure he didn't have a refrigerator.

I followed him so I could unravel the mystery myself. It was a simple, yet puzzling solution; he had one of those miniature refrigerators that you usually see in college dorm rooms. It must have been underneath the myriad of books in his trailer. He kept it on his kitchen cabinet so he wouldn't have to break his back to access it.

"Why not buy a decent refrigerator?" I asked.

"I move around so much that I try to keep my belongings small and portable. I just found that this works best for my circumstances," he answered.

"How often do you move?"

"I've moved about twice every year for the last six years," he said nonchalantly.

"You in the military?" I thought was an obvious question.

"Nope. I just like to move around a lot. And I'm lucky enough to be able to afford it."

"What do you do?" I prompted again, with the gut feeling that he thought I was interrogating him, which, indeed, I was.

"I guess you could call me a Jack-of-all-trades. I'm a theologist, anthropologist, spermologist, and somewhat of a philosopher. Right now, however, I'm pretty much earning my keep with investments."

All I could get out was, "Wow! What, pray tell, is a spermologist?" and was immediately afraid that I shouldn't have asked.

"That is actually my specialty," he replied. "Not exactly like what it sounds. A spermologist is a collector of trivia. It's the best word I know of that describes my undying devotion to learning. I am constantly seeking information that I don't already know. It isn't a very acceptable way of making a living, however."

My curiosity got the best of me, and I challenged him to give me a sample.

"Very well," he smiled. "Continuing on the same vein we started yesterday; did you know that ants outnumber humans one-million to one?"

"No, I didn't," I replied truthfully.

"Well they do, and up until last night I didn't either. I did a bit of math to try to put some perspective on that, and I came up with the following numbers," he said as he handed me a sheet of paper that was sitting on his kitchen cabinet. It looked like this:

$$6,500,000,000 * 1,000,000 = 6,500,000,000,000,000$$
Assuming 1/8" per ant: $8 * 12 * 5280 = 506,880$ ants per mile
$$6,500,000,000,000,000 / 506,880 = 12,823,547,979 \text{ miles}$$
$$12,823,547,979 \text{ miles} / 93,000,000 \text{ miles} =$$
137.8876 times each way
$$137.8876 / 2 = 68.9438 \text{ round trips}$$

I looked at it for a moment, shaking my head in dismay for not grasping what it was that he was imparting to me. The silence that existed while I was looking at the numbers was somewhat disturbing. I was afraid he was waiting for the light to come on and me to figure out the grand scheme of things from this diagram. That wasn't going to happen; not at 7:00 on a Saturday morning. After what seemed like 20 minutes, I shook my head again and said, "Alright, I give up. What does this mean?"

Pointing at the paper, he slowly made his way across each line. "There are roughly 6 and a half billion humans on the Earth right now. Ants outnumber humans 1 million to one. 6.5 billion times 1 million equals 6.5 quadrillion."

So far I was following his logic.

He then moved to the next line and continued, "Assuming that the average ant is 1/8 of an inch long, (and this is a big assumption; the average ant is probably much longer than 1/8 of an inch), there are 8 ants to an inch, 12 inches per foot, 5280 feet per mile. 8 times 12 times 5280 equals 506,880 ants per mile."

I still had no problem following his logic.

Moving to the next line I began to see where he was headed with this. "6.5 quadrillion ants divided by 506,880 ants per mile equals 12,823,547,979 miles. So, roughly, if you take all the ants on the Earth today and place them end to end, like they were going to a big picnic, they would stretch for 12,823,547,979 miles. The next two lines I calculated for reference. The sun is roughly 93 million miles from the Earth. 12,823,547,979 miles divided by 93,000,000 miles = 137.8876 times (going one way). This means that these same ants, if they were headed to the sun and back, could make the trip almost 69 times."

I stood stupefied. Ants going to the sun and back 69 times. How should I respond to that? Albeit, it was fascinating, but was it true? I highly doubted it. The math seemed right, it just didn't seem like the Earth was large enough to hold something that big. The only line I could really even see that might be a problem was the ratio of ants per humans. Everything else I knew was a fairly good approximation.

"By the way," he added, "most people don't know the series of large numbers that follow a trillion. It's actually quite easy to understand, if you know a little Greek. All you have to do is count to ten using Greek prefixes. Million = 1, Billion = 2, Trillion = 3, Quadrillion = 4, Quintillion = 5, Sextillion = 6, Septillion = 7, Octillion = 8, Nonillion = 9, and Decillion = 10. I'm not sure what use this would be to you, but it's interesting to know."

My head was becoming woozy. I needed to sit down, but there was no chair in sight. Out of the corner of my eye I caught the green-ribboned package I had placed on the counter when I traded it for the glass of orange juice and the calculations. My head began to clear: now back to reality.

"I got you a housewarming gift," I blurted as I lifted the present from the counter to his hands in one swift move. "I thought you might enjoy this."

He started to say something, but stopped himself after a low guttural utterance. He peered at the package and gingerly removed the bow. An extremely faint smile dawned his lips as he entered what can only be described as a very somber mood. Slowly he turned the package over and began glossing the directions on the back of the box, but he didn't make it all the way through them. I know this because his eyes were too moist. He didn't say a word. I felt awkward. The awkwardness increased as he quietly set the box on the counter and embraced me with both arms.

"Thank you," he sobbed. "Thank you."

5.
POPPING THE QUESTION

Stepping into our home I was greeted by my wife, still in her bathrobe. She's Norwegian, but there are moments when I think she bears a strong resemblance to the Swiss Miss Cocoa Girl. She looks young and takes good care of herself. She has a natural beauty that doesn't require much, if any, makeup, but that doesn't seem to stop her from spending a long time in front of the mirror. I never could understand why I could make it from the bed to being fully dressed in the time it takes her to turn her curling iron on. Maybe it has something to do with the fact that I'm fat and bald and don't really care what I look like. I'm pretty sure she married me for my sense of humor, because there's no way it was for my looks or money – I don't have any of either, and the prospects seem to be getting worse every day. Maybe she was just desperate.

The home was warm with the smell of bacon, which provided a sharp contrast to the musty smell I had just left behind.

"I saved you some," she said, reading my thoughts as she typically does. "You guys have a squirt gun fight or something?" she asked, as she pointed to the tearstains on my shoulder.

I told her of the gift bearing session and the warm reception it provoked. She tilted her head to the side a bit and 'hmmm'd' to herself. I could tell she was concocting a plan. I have to admit it was a good one, though.

"Maybe we should ask him over tonight with the others," she said.

Saturday night, of course, I thought, the party. We had invited three couples over for hors d' oeuvres and games. "That's a great idea," I replied. And then added "But he'd feel out of place if he's the only single guy here."

"Are you kidding?" she responded quickly. "You guys don't give the women a second look once the party starts, anyway. If he knows anything about football, ignoring women, and stuffing his face, he'll blend right in."

"You've got a point," I acknowledged. "Let's go the extra mile to make sure he fits in. I'll see if we can find a game of Trivial Pursuit to play. He told me he's a 'spermologist', maybe we can put that to the test tonight."

After a brief explanation that that was not a dirty word, I called to my youngest daughter Valerie to come do me a favor. I had an inclination that if I were to invite JP to the party myself, the invitation would be gracefully declined. But there was no way he would be able to reject my blue-eyed, heart-melting six year old daughter.

I gave her instructions and made her repeat them to me to convince myself that she remembered them. I patted the back of her head as she skittered down the driveway en route to JP's house. I quickly snatched the hose from off of the front lawn and pretended that I was watering the weed patch that we call our flowerbed. What I heard of the conversation went to perfection. It went something like this:

"My Dad says you're invited to a party at our house tonight at 8:00. Wear comfortable clothes and bring a bag of potato chips. He won't take 'no' for an answer. Goodbye."

As she started to walk away, I heard him ask her to wait just a minute. I saw his reflection in our front window as he stepped back into his house and bolted through his living room into his kitchen. He was back in a flash. I saw him bend over and hand something to my daughter. He bent over still further and whispered something in her ear. She gave a polite "Thank you" and turned to make her way back across the street. I was pleased as she looked both ways before crossing.

"Look what JP gave me Daddy," she said, holding up a piece of chewing gum. "JP said he'd be happy to come."

She bounded up the stairs and threw open the door. "Oh," she added, "he also said to tell you that the hose works better if you turn it on."

I looked down at the dry hose in my hand and winced with embarrassment. I glanced over my shoulder just in time to see JP chuckling to himself as he closed his front door behind him.

6.
WITH WONDERING AWE

"Well, maybe the real God uses tricks.
Maybe He's not omnipotent,
He's just been around so long that He knows everything."
- Phil Connors (Bill Murray) from Groundhog Day (1993)

Locating a game of Trivial Pursuit turned out to be harder than I had expected. Gees, five years ago *everybody* had one. Now there were so many new versions I hardly recognized the game.

I scoured every house on our block looking for 'the original' – the one in the blue box. At long last I found it. Not on our block, of course, but at our backyard neighbor's. One look at the questions and I knew JP had met his match. None of that simple stuff, these were the brain-rackers. It made me more comfortable knowing he'd feel a little more in his own element. Advantage: JP.

About ten minutes to eight I selected five CD's from my collection and loaded them in our CD player. In general, I picked good background music that wouldn't overpower conversation. I selected the 'shuffle' option and tapped the play button. The volume was a titch too high so I turned it down. Perfect.

The doorbell chimed. Let the party begin. It was Rob and Natalie Call. It didn't surprise me that they were the first to arrive; we had been best friends for over a year, and they didn't care if they shattered the precedent of being fashionably late. I made a remark that Rob looked as hairy as ever and he took a mock swing at me. We had that type of relationship. There were little or no secrets between the two of us. If I thought it, I'd say it to him; and vice versa.

We'd talk about anything. We shot the bull for a couple of minutes while we waited for the other couples to arrive.

The Dalfonso's were next. Steve and Claudia. Steve and I worked together and were one of the few daring programmer's to actually have a sense of humor. I'd never met his wife. She was Asian and had a great smile. She acted shy at first, but as the night went on she opened up.

The Gunnell's brought up the anchor position. Scott was also a programmer and added a Bob Newhart touch to the humor Steve and I provided. As I made the necessary introductions, I noticed that Desiree seemed uncomfortable, and later I found out why: she had dated Rob Call in high school and hadn't seen him since. (What are the odds?)

On the Gunnell's coattails was the man of the hour. He was draped in a baggy tie-dyed shirt with three-quarter length sleeves. I almost blurted out that the sixties had ended over twenty years ago, but stopped myself because I didn't know how well he'd receive it. Stopping myself from saying something that might be construed as being funny is not what I would normally do. I spend a fair amount of time retrieving my foot from my mouth.

I welcomed JP with a warm handshake and ushered him in to our living room where the other couples, who already knew each other, sat in animated conversation. I made introductions, as necessary. I gestured to the kitchen and invited all to load up a plate. I watched in horror as seven ravenous wolves attacked the hors d' oeuvres.

JP was the odd man out. At first it concerned me a bit, until I saw he was headed for the stereo speaker. He ducked his head down to get closer to the speaker and gently closed his eyes as I watched his body melt into the music. It was Bruce Hornsby's version of the John Lennon classic Imagine. The final verse had just begun, and I had the distinct impression that I had robbed him of the previous two. It was so odd to see someone so absorbed in space. Chills shot down my backbone. The two of us got lost in time. Him, because of the music, me because watching him reminded me of, something, I couldn't put my finger on what it was.

As the final piano roll echoed to a close, he turned and stated, "Bruce Hornsby. I never heard that version."

"You like Hornsby?" I asked.

"I like music," was his poignant reply.

"We need to get together. I'm somewhat of a music lover myself. Grab some grub. Let's get this party started. After you," I said, holding up a plate for him.

It was not my intention to spend the entire evening playing Trivial Pursuit, but as it turned out, that's what happened. Somehow it always works out that women think they can outthink men; and tonight was no exception. Gwen, Claudia, Desiree and Natalie all huddled on one side of the room and dared us to take them on. The five men looked at each other as if to say, "Who do they think they're kidding?" as we cracked our knuckles and scratched our privates to demonstrate that our superior testosterone levels would once again prove that male domination happens for a reason.

JP, however, quietly bowed out of the action by volunteering himself to be the official moderator and reader of questions. I didn't like the idea, because I thought it isolated him, and worse yet, wouldn't allow him to demonstrate his true character as a spermologist. He was fairly persistent, however, and finally we all reluctantly gave in.

The night flew by with a generous blend of story telling and laughter, with an occasional correct answer provided for gaming purposes. It took us about an hour and a half for each side to acquire four pieces of pie. The game was certainly not the center of attention at any given moment, but I don't think anyone cared. We were enjoying ourselves.

I peered across the taupe Berber carpet and caught my wife's gaze. It always seems like the most seductive of situations happen when you are buried in background conversation and both time and distance separate you. This was just such a situation. Her green eyes glowed like she could see right through me. She gestured toward the kitchen to me with her head. I snagged some of the discarded paper plates from off of the floor and followed after her.

I was prepared for her to make a vocal pass at me, so her comment caught me off guard: "Have you noticed JP?"

"Noticed what?" I asked worriedly, wondering whether he'd left his fly open or something.

"To my knowledge, he hasn't flipped a card over to look at an answer yet."

"What are you talking about? He's been giving us the answers all night."

"Yes," she said slyly. "But he hasn't been *looking* at the answers. Check it out."

After whispering some random sweet nothings in her ear and nibbling at the base of her neck, I grabbed a few cucumbers and dip and followed her back to the living room. I was anxious to see what this was all about.

The women had a history question. I watched as JP dipped into the box of cards and cupped his hand around the back of the first one as he slid it from the container.

For the first time since we'd met, I took a good look at his features. His deep saddened eyes missed nothing as he took everything in. Although he didn't participate in our dialogue much, he was ready at the drop of a hat to pitch in a comment or two, always pertinent, always insightful. He seemed to be more at ease when he was watching, rather than participating, and I don't think it was just because he was in unfamiliar territory.

His square shoulders never slouched, and he held his head high although he couldn't have been more than 5'9". He held his right forearm against his abdomen. I wondered whether he had ever had surgery on his right elbow. I'd never seen anyone carry their arm like that before, unless they had it in a sling. There didn't seem to be any pain involved in his movements, however.

There was something weathered about him that suggested he'd been through the ropes a time or two. I was certain I was staring at a very lonely man, although I couldn't understand why, the women in the group found him quite pleasant 'eye-candy', as my wife puts it.

My thoughts were cut short by JP's voice reading the next question.

"What assassin is due for release on February 28, 1986?"

The ladies huddled together and I heard a few names slung around, but nothing that had any semblance of certainty behind it. Finally, they came up with a name that I probably would have guessed:

"Charles Manson," chimed their collective guess.

"Sirhan Sirhan," JP retorted as he slid the card in the back of the box. Then muttered under his breath "No pie for you."

He had not looked at the back of the card. Gwen and I shot a quizzical glance at each other while both sides of the room made various comments. I shrugged my shoulders and jutted my chin toward him to indicate that I wanted to hear a few more questions before I made any hasty judgments.

I marveled as he rifled through the next six cards without looking at the back of any of them. To compound the absurdity of the matter, between the two teams, we hadn't gotten any of the questions correct. Yet, if what I was witnessing was legitimate, JP didn't even need to look at the correct answer to know the answer. Now it was the men's turn. At this juncture, I was more involved with the sideshow than the main event.

Geography: "What U.S. state contains the geographic center of North America?" was the question. I noted his unwavering hand shielding the answers. His eyes, did however, slightly glance up as if he actually had to visualize this one.

We tossed around a few logical answers and finally concluded that the answer must be Kansas. We all echoed that sentiment together.

"That is incorrect. The correct answer is North Dakota," he responded, once again sliding the card to the back of the stack without looking at it.

This was too much. Although I wouldn't swear that the geographic center of the United States was Kansas, I knew darn well it wasn't North Dakota. This guy had to be exposed. I arose in my typical Type 'A' fashion and I addressed my audience; time for some real fun.

"This man," I said, exaggerating an accusing finger in JP's direction, "although providing us with answers, has not looked at the correct answer for at least eight questions. My intuition tells me that he is concocting false answers and passing them off as the true and real answers. This man is a fraud!"

I snatched the box of cards from his lap and snared the final card from the deck. "And the *correct* answer is…" I glossed the back of the card for the right answer. "No way," I muttered, shaking my head in disbelief - "North Dakota."

As both sides of the room cackled in hysterics over my disillusionment, I rifled hysterically through the previous seven cards in the deck, verifying the authenticity of his answers. My eighth and final wallop came with the historical question having an answer 'Sirhan Sirhan.' He was eight for eight. The collective eight of us were zero for eight on the same questions. He'd been beating us all night, and we hadn't even noticed he'd been playing.

"You misunderstood the question," he grinned. "They're not asking for the geographic center of the *United States*, they're looking for the geographic center of *North America*."

It took several seconds for the rest of the group to catch on to the brilliance that we were witnessing; but catch on it did. As a matter of fact, it ignited. From that moment on, it became a contest of who could stump JP. We took turns rummaging through the cards and reading every question on the card. With uncanny accuracy, he spat out the correct answer before we could even locate it on the back of the card.

At one point the eight of us collectively selected six cards, each having a category of what we perceived to be the hardest question we could find. He went six for six, although he did actually have to pause a moment to consider one of two options on the Entertainment question.

As the wee hours of the morning approached, we became convinced that JP was unstumpable. It was frustrating that we couldn't come up with anything he *didn't* know. While glancing at the open box that lay sprawled on the floor, I came up with an idea.

"Who holds the copyright for Trivial Pursuit?" I leered.

Without hesitation, he flabbergasted me: "Horn Abbot Ltd, 1981."

I passed around the box so that all could see he was, once again, precise in his answer. The eight of us stood there gawking at him as if he were inhuman.

He arose, brushing his shirt with his hands as he did. "I'm very tired. I've had a great time. It's been a pleasure meeting you all."

There were some collective protests from the peanut gallery, but he persisted, and eventually we allowed him to leave. If it were up to us, we'd have kept him captive 'til sun up.

As I walked him to the door he was chuckling to himself. We stood cross-armed on the front porch not really knowing what to say while echoes of bewildered conversations floated through the door.

"You think they think I'm a freak?" he asked, genuinely concerned.

"Man, even I think you're a freak," I responded. "But an incredibly smart one."

"I have a confession to make," he confided. "The last question you asked, the one about the copyright..."

"Go on," I urged.

A smirk dawned on his otherwise serious face. "I noticed it on the box while I was taking the questions out of it. I wouldn't have known that answer, otherwise."

I scoffed at his modesty. "But even to remember it after all the questions we fired at you is pretty impressive," I offered.

"Even so," he said, "I feel like I cheated on that one."

"I'll let the others know, but I doubt it will mar your reputation. You didn't cheat on the other questions, did you?"

"No. I knew the answers on the rest."

"Well then, you are by far the most intelligent person I know," I nodded confidently.

"Don't confuse intelligence with the ability to regurgitate trivia. Intelligence requires application. Trivia is just that – trivia. Not much application involved in true trivia."

"I guess," I conceded, not really following due to the lateness of the hour. "Thanks for coming, you were truly impressive. Please allow me to apologize for questioning your intellect."

"It was a pleasure being here. Thanks for having me. And I don't blame you for acting the way you did. Apology accepted."

And with that he strode through the darkness to his home, leaving the eight of us to ponder whether or not what we had just witnessed was real.

7.
POINTS OF VIEW

"The test of a first-rate intelligence is the ability to hold two opposing ideas in mind at the same time and still retain the ability to function."
- F. Scott Fitzgerald (1896 – 1940)

It was a full forty hours before I saw him again. The truth of the matter was that I liked being around him. There was an electricity about him that made me start thinking on a higher plane than I ever had before. It was contagious, and the aura of mystery that had surrounded him the other night only added to my intrigue. Gwen took notice of the fact that I was frequently in Never-Never land. I confided in her that I couldn't stop thinking about our new neighbor; that he fascinated me. To my surprise, she too, seemed intrigued, and rather than discouraging my interest, suggested that I take him some cookies that she'd made that afternoon. I leapt at the opportunity to see him again.

After piling a paper plate with semi-sweet chocolate chip cookies, I lunged for the door and across the street. As I strode past the murky green 1969 Rambler in his driveway, I locked in on the Florida plates that had piqued my curiosity enough to enlist the cops in helping to 'uncovering' him. I felt a wave of guilt sweep over me for having been so pessimistic. As my mind wandered to the events that had transpired over the course of the last four days, I heard the clack of a dead bolt being unlocked and the swooshing of a door being pulled open from the inside. It's as if he had been waiting for me.

"Welcome, neighbor!"

"Howdy. My wife thought you might like some cookies."

His face contorted as he bellowed, "Are you passing them around the whole neighborhood, or are all those for me?"

"She made plenty. This didn't even make a dent in them," I said. "And knowing my wife, she's probably pretty happy to get them out of the house so she doesn't eat 'em all herself."

"They look great, and I could use an extra pound or two," he said as he grabbed his gut and shook it a bit. In reality, there was nothing there to grab, this guy took good care of himself. He hoisted an index finger in my direction and declared, "Hang on a second, I'll be right back."

He hustled back into his house and left the door slightly ajar. I heard some banging coming from within as he did whatever it was that he was doing. Moments later, he returned brandishing two steel folding chairs. He flicked them open with a quick snap of the wrist and set them about seven feet apart on the front porch, facing my house.

"Nice evening," he gestured toward the sky. "You got some time to kill?"

"Sure. Actually, that's what I came over here for. I've got some things that've been running through my mind that I'd like to talk to you about."

"Shoot!" he said, turning his chair around and resting his broad forearms on the backrest as he planted himself in the seat.

"Well, the other night at the party you were awesome. It's just been nagging at me how somebody gets so smart. Where'd you learn all that stuff?"

"I get around," he said slowly, almost to himself. "I guess I just have a knack for remembering things that most people don't have."

"That's an understatement," I scoffed. "So where all have you been?"

"There's very few places I haven't been," he reminisced. "The only continents I haven't set foot on are

Australia and Antarctica. And I'd love to go to either of those, or both."

"Wow!" I shirked. "How does someone as young as you get around so much? Was your dad in the military?"

A glazed look swept over his face, almost as if he didn't understand my question. He shook his head slowly, as if to both clear his head of cobwebs, and answer my question at the same time.

"No. I just enjoy seeing new places and taking it all in. I'm fortunate enough to have sufficient money stored away to finance my travels."

Once again he rose and made his way to the door. "Hang on a second. I've got something you might enjoy."

He returned with a roughly hewn overgrown wooden cup, (or was it a bowl?), that had several small chips of wood, almost splinters, lying within it. He gently placed it on my lap as if it were a prized trophy. He brandished a sense of pride with whatever it was he had just bestowed upon me. As for me, I couldn't quite make out what I should think of it.

"Quiz me," he said.

"Alright," I agreed, playing along.

I dipped my hand in the cup and pulled out one of the splinters of wood.

"What is this?" I asked, holding it up like a poker chip for him to see.

"A piece of teak, or possibly oak, from the deck of the USS West Point," he gleamed.

I took a closer look at it, as if I could discern the authenticity of his answer. Nope - I couldn't.

"And this?" I said, reaching for another fragment of wood.

"A remnant of palm from the rocky Northern shores of Madagascar."

"And this?" I continued.

"A twig off of an Olive tree, from the Middle East."

I held up another.

"Gingko, from Northern Asia."

I pulled out the two remaining pieces at the same time, cupping them both in my right hand.

"The one on the left is Cedar, from a fishing boat, also in the Middle East. The one on the right, a small token of the mighty Baobab, from Central Africa."

"Man, you *do* get around," I noted. "Kind of an unusual collection. Did you collect all of these yourself?"

He reached over and removed the cup from my lap, then gently placed the chips back into the bottom of it. He cradled it like a newborn.

"Yes," he replied. "To anyone else these are nothing. To me, they represent my life; where I've been."

"So your body of knowledge is based on experience?" I asked.

"Yes and no. I get around, but I read an awful lot, too. You name a book and I've probably read it."

"So, what's your favorite continent?" I grinned, knowing it was a rhetorical question.

"Apples and oranges," he replied. "There's no way to compare them."

"What's the major difference?" I asked.

"Well, beside the obvious lifestyle differences, the way of thinking is completely different. People have different mind-sets. In general, Westerners think in terms of 'either / or', while Easterners think in non-contradictory terms."

"I'm not following you," I said, feeling stupid.

"Well," he continued, stooping to my level, "I once heard two ministers of different religions arguing. Their argument went something like this:

Minister 1: 'Either you are right, or I am
right. We cannot both be right.'
Minister 2: 'I agree.'

"I didn't even hear what they were arguing about,
but the thought that immediately crossed my mind was: No,
there is a third option: you both could be wrong. And then I
drew another conclusion: perhaps both of you are partially
right.

"Westerners feel that every question and issue must
have either a 'right or wrong' answer. There is no middle
ground. Easterners, on the other hand, hear both extremes
and find a happy medium. It allows for less controversy and
more compromise."

"I see," I said, and I did see. "So which way of
thinking do you subscribe to?"

"See what I mean?" he gloated. "With Westerners,
it's got to be one or the other. But to answer your question, I
use both. I try to be open minded about most things, but
there are some issues that require the 'either / or' type of
reasoning. I must admit though, that I believe the culture
spawned the ideal. Western lifestyle is very high stress when
contrasted to the Eastern lifestyle."

"I'd love to travel," I said, hoping the conversation
would proceed to something a little lighter.

"It's great for a while, but it gets old fast if you're
not ready for it. You're lucky enough to be able to stay put.
You've got a good thing going here," he nodded toward my
house.

"Yes I do," I agreed, feeling somewhat guilty for
taking it for granted.

And right on cue my youngest daughter Valerie
stuck her head out the door and shouted, "Mommy said to
tell you it's time for dinner."

I rose and thanked him for his time.

"Any time," he replied. And I knew I'd take him up
on that offer.

He thanked me for the cookies, and we said our 'goodbyes' As I strolled across the street to our house, I wondered whether dinner would be something I loved, or something I couldn't stand, because it had to be one or the other.

8.
THE JOKER

As is the case with most people, I am a creature of habit. It was around this time that I made an every day routine of doing the 8:00 to 5:00, coming home and giving the wife and kids a hug and peck on the cheek, and then heading over to JP's for a half hour or so until dinner was ready. His schedule must have jived with mine, because he was always there on his front porch waiting for me. I'd always return home in time for dinner. After dinner, I'd spend the rest of the evening with the family, or reading. In general, the less it involved the television set, the happier I was.

My wife enjoyed staying home during the days, and I made a decent salary, so I had no complaints. We made ends meet with room to spare each month. The kids seemed to like having their Mother at home to look after them. She'd noticed a big change in their behavior; not that they were bad before, it just seemed they showed more respect to each other if she was around more often.

So I'd come home and throw on some jeans and a T-shirt, and meander across the street to where JP was always patiently waiting for me. I loved that porch. It faced south, so we were shaded from the early evening sun. This may sound odd, but I liked looking at my own home from a neighbor's perspective. It allowed me to step out of the rut I had previously been in and [seemingly] look at my life from the outside. Those thirty minutes of each day were typically the highlight of the entire day.

Our conversations covered a myriad of topics, but invariably led to the brain in one way or another. The major reason for this was the fact that I was in almost every way JP's protégé, and he was my mentor. He did all that he could do to level our ways of thinking, and I certainly wasn't fighting the issue. I would ask boatloads of questions, and JP would provide answers, usually mingled with some sort of moral to the story, if at all possible. It's odd, but his morals never seemed to sink in until after I'd had some time to reflect on what he was saying.

"You ready for some intellectual humor?" he asked one day.

"Sure."

"I gotta warn you, my humor is not like most people's."

"Try me," I said.

"There was once a man who searched high and low for the secret of life. He had been to all of the great philosophers and theologians in several different countries; and none of them could provide him with a concise definition to the secret of life. After a lifelong search had proved fruitless, he finally came upon a man who said that he himself didn't know the secret of life, but that he knew a man who did know the secret of life. If he visited that man, he was sure he would tell him. He gave him instructions on how and where to find this man and sent him on his way.

"The man was thrilled to know that his lifelong pursuit was about to be fulfilled. He sold most of his worldly possessions and bought a plane ticket to Tibet and hired men to escort him through the Himalayas to the home of this great Guru who knew the secret of life.

"Chills ran down his spine as he entered into the meager shack of the Guru. He removed his shoes and reverently bowed his head to the Guru and asked: 'Oh, great Guru, I have searched high and low for the secret of life and I have been told that you know of it. Please tell it to me so that I, too, may share in this great secret.'

"The great Guru bowed in reverence to the mans devotion and said, 'I would be honored to tell you this great secret. It is this: To enjoy life to its fullest, you must get along with everyone by agreeing with everything that they say.'

"The man sat in wonder for a moment, and then shook his head in disbelief at the time and effort he had wasted, searching for this nugget of truth that he deemed to be ridiculous. 'That's ludicrous!' he shouted. 'That's the stupidest thing I've ever heard.'

"To which the Guru replied, 'You are absolutely right.'"

I waited for a moment for him to present the punch line; but he had already given it. The joke was over. He sat there with a smirk on his face like I was supposed to think it was the funniest thing I'd ever heard. It wasn't.

"You may find it to be more funny as time wears on," he added hopefully. "I think it's rather profound, myself."

"I guess when you said you were going to tell me a joke, I assumed I was going to hear something funny," I chuckled.

He too, chuckled at my remark. "Now that reminds me of another joke."

"Is this one funny?" I asked, genuinely concerned.

"It's funnier than the last one," he chortled.

"It'd be hard not to be. Okay, one more try," I conceded.

He inhaled deeply and formulated his thoughts. I could tell he wanted this one to come out better than the last.

"It was a man's first night in prison. He had spent the day feeling extremely depressed. The warden yelled 'Lights out!' and the lights clicked off. As the man sat there contemplating how lonely and dejected he was, the silence was broken by someone yelling, 'Seventy-two!' and all the inmates laughing.

"'Fifty-one!' someone else yelled, again to a chorus of laughter.

"This continued for about twenty minutes, with people yelling out seemingly random numbers, echoed by a barrage of laughter. Finally the humor died down and everyone went to sleep.

"The next day, the man inquired of a fellow inmate what all the commotion was at bedtime the previous evening. He was informed that all of the inmates passed around a list of everyone's favorite jokes. Instead of telling the joke repeatedly, the inmates just numbered the jokes and memorized which joke belonged to which number. Every night at bedtime they would all tell their favorite jokes by reciting the number beside the joke.

"So the man acquired a list of the jokes and spent several days reading and memorizing them. He found his favorite and prepared to join in the fun that night. Sure enough, the lights went out and the numbers started flying. The man was tense. Then during a slight lull in the joke telling, he blurted it out: 'Thirty-eight!' he yelled triumphantly. Much to his dismay, there was dead silence. 'Thirty-eight!' he hollered again. And once again it aroused no reception whatsoever. Then, through the silence, he heard someone mutter, 'Some people just don't know how to tell a good joke.'"

This one drew a snicker from me, although it was far from a belly-buster. "You probably ought to stick to trivia," I said. "Because your future as a comedian just isn't gonna fly."

"I tried," he hung his head in mock shame.

"And a gallant effort it was," I added.

He nodded in agreement and we sat in reflective silence until I went home for supper.

9.
THE "A-HA" PRINCIPLE

We're two of a kind, silence and I, we need a chance to talk things over.
Two of a kind, silence and I, we'll find a way to work it out.
- From <u>Silence and I</u> by The Alan Parsons Project (1982)

My favorite of all the stories that JP related to me was of the great mathematician Archimedes. The main reason for that was because of its applicability: I used it every day at my office.

As always, it began on the front porch of his house in those incredibly uncomfortable folding steel chairs. (Maybe there was a reason he always sat backwards.)

"You ever heard of Archimedes?" he began.

"Heard the name, but don't know anything about him," I replied.

"Archimedes was one of the greatest mathematicians that ever lived. Although he was born around 290 B.C., he came up with many concepts we still use in our everyday life today; such as the lever, and the rule of buoyancy."

"I've heard of those. I just didn't know where they originated," I said.

"Archimedes' principle of buoyancy states that any object completely or partially submerged in a fluid is acted upon by an upward force that is equal to the weight of the fluid displaced by that object. Or, more simply stated, when you put a lump of butter in a cup of water, the weight of the displaced water equals the weight of the lump of butter. But it's the story behind the story that I think is interesting."

He continued: "Around 250 B.C., a certain Hiero, the King of Syracuse, and Archimedes' close friend, commissioned a goldsmith to fashion a crown of pure gold that would be placed atop a statue in honor of the gods. The precise dimensions of the crown were given to the goldsmith, along with the solid gold ingots to be melted down and used in the crown. After the crown had been completed, the King suspected he had been swindled, but didn't know how he could prove it. He assigned Archimedes to the task. To complicate the matter, Hiero instructed Archimedes that since the crown was a gift to the gods', it could not be destroyed in any way.

"For several days Archimedes labored over a way to prove or disprove the King's theory of the fraudulent crown. Finally, after several days of what must have been mind-racking labor, Archimedes literally threw in the towel. He stopped working on the problem altogether, and retired to the public bathhouse for a much needed rest.

"While stripping himself of his clothes and stepping into a bath, he happened to glance at the edge of the bathtub, and noticed that the water level rose proportionately as he lowered himself into it. He was so overcome with delight that he ran naked through the streets of Syracuse, screaming 'Eureka! Eureka!' which means, 'I found it! I found it!'

"After he regained his composure and donned some clothes, he presented the solution to Hiero. That is: he would place a gold ingot known to be the exact weight of that required in the crown in a bowl of water filled to the brim. The gold ingot would then be removed, and the crown, suspected of being fraudulent, would be placed in the same bowl of water. If the water rose precisely to the top of the bowl, the crown would be proven to have the identical composition of the gold ingot. If not, the crown would be proven fraudulent.

"The test was conducted, and the crown was, indeed, proven to be fraudulent. The goldsmith was beheaded for his misdeed, and Archimedes' principle of buoyancy had been born."

"So what's the moral of the story?" I daunted.

"There are three that I can think of. The first, is don't mess with the King.

"The second: Archimedes rule of buoyancy.

"The third, and lesser known moral, is that the brain communicates to us in ways and at times that we can't even begin to imagine. Archimedes' consciously struggled for days trying to solve a problem, but it was his subconscious mind that actually came up with the solution *only after he had decided to let his mind rest from the problem.* I am a firm subscriber to the notion that if we initially feed our brain with all of the information it needs to solve a problem, the solution will come to us in due course at a time when we might least expect it, possibly even when we're not concentrating directly on the problem itself. Many of the great concepts of our time were conceived while the author was relaxing, or even asleep. I think it's very possible to think about a problem for too long, and this story is a good demonstration of that."

"Interesting," I acknowledged, while letting the concept sink in.

"You ever have problems at work that take you days to solve?" he asked.

"Not really days," I answered. "But there have been times when I've sat for hours debugging a program, only to discover that a single period was in the wrong place, causing completely unexpected results."

"Well, there's a reason breaks were introduced in the workplace. The next time you come across a seemingly unsolvable problem, try taking a break. It's amazing how often you'll solve the problem while you are purposely trying to avoid it altogether," he said.

"You 'think outside the box' a lot, don't you?" I observed.

"It's what I do best," he confided.

10.
THE THUNDER OF SILENCE

"True friendship comes when silence between two
people is comfortable."
-    Dave Tyson Gentry

"I want to continue with the concept we started
yesterday," he began. "I once had a teacher that confided in
me what he deemed to be one of the most important, yet
relatively unknown, aspects of teaching. He taught me, in
one simple idea, how to be an effective teacher."

"And how's that?" I asked.

"He told me of a woman named Mary Budd Rowe
from Stanford University who conducted a survey among
one hundred teachers that had been selected by their
students as the most effective teachers. Now, by the word
'effective', I don't necessarily mean they were the most
liked, or the funniest, but they were the ones that *taught* the
best. The students learned the most from them."

"Go on," I urged.

"The surveyors sat with the teachers during their
respective lessons, and took notes on their teaching methods
to see if they could uncover any secrets as to what makes an
effective teacher. After the surveys had been taken, the
notes were itemized, and without exception, one quality rose
to the top as the most consistently used by almost all of the
truly effective teachers. Care to take a guess as to what this
quality was?" he tested me.

I contemplated the question and tossed forth my best
guess: "They cared," I offered.

"Try again," he prodded.

"They were well prepared," I tried.

"Nope."

"They were interesting to listen to."

"All important things," he said, "but not the common denominator. The one thing that every one of these teachers had in common was open-ended questions followed by a noticeable moment of silence after every question they asked."

I reflected for a moment, and then responded, "That seems trivial."

"Yes it does," he said, "But think about it. If I ask you an open-ended question and immediately respond with the answer to that question, it allows you no time to think, no time to come up with a solution on your own. Too often students are bludgeoned with information and not allowed time for the brain to engage. If time is allowed for the brain to process information on its own accord, it forces individual thought, and even if incorrect conclusions are drawn, at least we know that the student was thinking.

"Miss Rowe found that the average teacher waited between .7 and 1.4 seconds after each question they asked. She concluded that the average teacher *should* wait at least twice that long, between 3 and 5 seconds, depending on the question. This aids the learning process by forcing the student to apply, rather than regurgitate.

"In cartoons, you frequently see this wait time drawn as a light bulb over someone's head. I think that's a pretty accurate depiction of this whole concept. It's the precise moment when the brain tells the body 'A-ha – I've got the answer'.

"And," he continued, "there is a second moment of silence that can be utilized when an *incorrect* answer is given to a question. Rather than blurting out that a student's answer is wrong, try pausing for a moment instead, and see if the student can correct himself without being told he's wrong. This method doubly reinforces the learning process.

"Here's an example," he said, applying the concept. "Tell me what you know about Einstein's theory of relativity."

And before I had a chance to think about it, he blurted out, "It's an equation demonstrating the relationship of mass to energy, isn't it?"

Suddenly the open-ended question that had begun in my mind had been replaced with a simple answer that required absolutely no conscious effort on my part.

"Yes," I stammered.

It was frustrating. I immediately saw the truth in what he was saying. Yet, it's exactly how most teachers that I could recall had tried to teach me; and probably the way that I taught others.

"Now, what would you say is the total population of both China and India combined?" he asked.

My initial reaction was to wait until he provided me with the answer, but this time he let silence do the teaching. He sat there glaring at me in such a way as to make me uncomfortable. The silence was deafening. My mind raced. I knew China held roughly one fourth of the world's population, and that India was roughly the same. Quick, I thought, what's one fourth plus one fourth? That's one half. I proceeded to the next step. What's the world's population? He told me this before. I knew this: about six and a half billion, I recalled. My mind raced again. What's one half of six and a half billion? Three and a quarter billion. That was the answer.

"Three and a quarter billion," I announced proudly.

"Good," he said, checking his mental clock. "That took approximately four and a half seconds. Seemed like forever, didn't it?"

"Yeah," I said in disbelief. "You sure it didn't take any longer than that?"

"Absolutely. And the nice thing is, you came up with it on your own, and you're all the better for it. Furthermore," he added, "the silence following a question shows that you respect the student enough to listen to what he has to say, even if the correct answer is not given. It brings the teacher-student relationship down to a more personal level, and leaves the door open to further trust within the relationship."

As we sat there quietly, I let the message sink in. From that moment on, I tried to accept the fact that the silence between JP and me that invariably lingered in any given conversation we had was not necessarily a bad thing, but rather, an emphasis on something that I might be better off pondering for a while.

11.
THE ANTS ARRIVE

If I cried out loud over sorrows I've known
And the secrets I've heard
It would ease my mind someone sharing the load
But I won't breathe a word.
 -From Silence and I by The Alan Parsons Project (1982)

One afternoon, as I made my way up the stairs that I had become so familiar with, I immediately sensed that something was different: JP's porch was not arrayed with the usual steel chairs. About the time I hit the top stair, the door flung open and he stepped out with an unusually pleased grin on his weathered face.

"I've got something to show you," he chided, like a kid with a new toy. "Check this out."

We stepped into his living room and I followed his extended arm in the direction he indicated. There, on his hearth, like a shrine to the Almighty, was the Ant Farm I had given him a couple of weeks earlier.

"I got the ants in the mail today," he leered.

"Sweeeeeet," I hummed. "And what are the little buggers up to today?" I pondered as I crouched in for a closer look.

To my amazement, the ants had already joined forces and were tunneling through the sand, which resembled tiny white balls of Styrofoam. The once perfectly horizontal sand was now being formed into mountains by the tidbits accumulating from the ants' various trips to the surface and back. I stood there for a long moment reflecting how little I actually knew about the world around me; and how much I could learn by watching this tiny universe unfold before my eyes.

I caught JP's reflection on the plastic and noted that his disposition had changed dramatically since I arrived. He stood there with folded arms waiting for me to turn around. As I did, he took a deep breath, as if he were about to make a speech, and then he exhaled again. Apparently, it wasn't time for the speech at that exact moment. I knew whatever it was that he was about to say wasn't coming easy for him. Finally, he broke the silence with an unexpected statement.

He chose his words carefully. "I, uh, owe you an explanation."

I waited without remarking, because I knew that whatever I said wouldn't help him any.

"When you gave me this ant farm," he continued, "I acted a bit, rattled, I guess. I just wanted you to know why."

Again silence for a moment. Then, very slowly, punctuating each sentence and picking out the precise words, he continued.

"I'm not very adept at making and keeping friends. As a matter of fact, my friends have a way of dying, right about the time I realize what an asset they are to me. Sometimes it just catches up to me. When you gave me that ant farm," he said, "it was one of those times."

The silences were getting increasingly longer. I was going to urge him to continue, but I thought better of it. I was caught between a rock and a hard place. On the one hand, I had a man that I knew absolutely nothing about suddenly opening up to me. On the other, my track record showed that when I tried to glean information from him, he kept to himself. I chose the 'keep-my-mouth-shut-and-learn-something' option. I was pleased with the results, although I would have preferred more.

"My best friend was killed right in front of me when I was relatively young… My brother was killed shortly after that… and both my Mother and Father died soon after. After that, I took care of my best friend's mother for a short time until she too, died. I've been somewhat of a loner ever since. I don't like to talk about it; and to be frank; I'm not sure why I'm telling you this now. I just felt kind of awkward the other day when I hugged you, and I know you did, too. I just wanted you to know there was a lot more behind it than the ant farm; although I did appreciate it."

That was it. He went full circle from ant farm to life story to ant farm and I hadn't said a word. It was killing me not to ask him to expound, but once again, I went with the decision not to pry. The moment of truth had come and gone. I'd missed it.

"Well, hopefully these ants will keep you company," I said, in a lame attempt to console him. "And, I don't know if this means that much to you, but I plan on being here for a while. I'm not going anywhere."

"I'm glad," he echoed quietly. "It definitely means something to me."

We shook hands and I parted his presence that evening grateful to have gotten to know him better, but still acutely aware that there was still much more to be learned.

12.
THE ULTIMATE QUESTION

"It's not that I'm afraid to die.
I just don't want to be there when it happens."
- Woody Allen (1935 -)

"I mentioned death yesterday," he started, "and it reminded me of an interesting question that I would like to pose to you now. Are you ready to do some heavy-duty thinking?"

"Go for it," I dared.

"The question is simple, but the answer is not. Take your time and weigh the possibilities before you answer," he paused. "Here is the question: If I knew both the 'when' and the 'how' of your death, would you want me to tell you?"

I was stunned for a brief moment at the depth of the question. The first several seconds of the silence that followed was the sound of me getting my bearings on what exactly it was he had asked. After I was sure I understood the question correctly, I restated it to clarify. "You know *how* and *when* I'm going to die. Do I want you to tell me?"

He nodded in the affirmative, with a bit of an evil grin as he did.

My gut instinct was to respond "No", because I had actually pondered this question before, and that was the answer I had always come up with. But I decided he wouldn't be asking it if it were that easy. I rephrased the question in my mind to be: 'Why *wouldn't* I want to know when and how I was going to die?' I thought of two conceivable answers:

1) Because death scared me, and I would be forever dwelling on the date of my death, thus ruining my life; or

2) The mystery surrounding death
intrigued me, and living a mystery
makes life that much more exciting.

Then I took the other route. What benefits would
there be in knowing when and how I was going to die?

1) I could make the most of each day,
knowing that time was running out, (I
should be doing this anyway) and;
2) I could plan for the future, having
been informed of it. I could even take
out a life insurance policy on myself a
week before my death to secure my
family's future. (Would that be
considered insurance fraud? It would
be really tough to prove.)

Finally, I decided to stick with my gut and said
aloud, "No, I wouldn't want to know."
"A man of mystery, huh?" he read my mind.
I thought he was changing the subject as he followed
with the question, "Have you ever heard the saying, 'Live
each day as if it were your last?'"
"Sure," I replied.
"I don't like that saying," he said, to my surprise.
"Would you go to work tomorrow if you knew you were
going to die tomorrow night?"
"Not a chance," I scoffed. "I have enough trouble
going to work assuming I'm going to live."
"Well, if you lived every day as if it were your last,
you'd never go to work, would you?"
I laughed at the thought. Once again, he had a point.
"The saying only applies to your mental state, and
the relationships you choose to develop," he said. "But it
can't be applied to what you actually *do*. If it did, everyone

would spend their entire lives eating rich food and taking their kids to Disneyland."

Getting back to the original question, he asked, "Did you stop to consider how knowing the time of your death would affect your life?"

"Not in too much depth," I said.

He followed up, "It's easy to say that if you were going to die tomorrow, you'd make today count. But, take the opposite point of view. If you knew you weren't going to die until you were 90, you'd probably be more adventurous. Climbing Mt. Everest might be an option at the age of 60, if you knew you had 30 years left."

"Not if I knew I'd be trapped in a crevice of ice for the last thirty," I joked.

"Good point," he chuckled a bit, and then got quite serious. "The only definitive conclusion out of either answer you could give is: Knowing how and when your life was going to end would drastically change the way you live; regardless of whether your time remaining is short or long. Which begs the question, 'Why do we live the way we do?' To which a very simple answer is: 'Because we don't know when we're going to die.' I think everyone has an innate sense that they are immortal."

I thought about it for a moment and agreed with him.

"You haven't covered the 'how' portion of your question, though," I noted.

This caught him off guard. "What do you mean?" he asked.

"Well, your initial question involved both when and *how* I was going to die. It seems to me that the 'fear' portion of death is at least partially covered by *how* we die. And knowing how we die would certainly affect the way we live."

He suddenly became keenly aware that I was smarter than he gave me credit for. He grinned and nodded courteously, "Please continue."

"Well, let's say you tell me that I'm going to drown, but you don't tell me *when* I'm going to drown. In all probability, I would avoid swimming pools and large bodies of water for the rest of my life in an effort to postpone my death. But if what you told me was inevitable, I might very well drown as I drank a glass of milk while watching from the shore as the rest of my family was playing in the ocean."

"Well put," he mused.

"So," I summarized, "it can be truly said that the more we know about our death, the more we alter our lives."

I grinned from ear to ear as I realized that I had actually said something that contributed to our conversation. I was on a roll. I decided to get his take on the question:

"How about you?" I asked. "Would you want to know when and how you were going to die?"

"Definitely not," he said, and then lulled off in to silence.

"A man of mystery," I mused. I liked this guy.

13.
LIFE AFTER LIFE

I know all your life you've wondered
About that step we all take alone.
How far does the spirit travel on the journey?
You must surely be near heaven.
And it thrills me to the bone,
To know Daddy knows the great unknown.
- April 24, 1981 from "Success Hasn't Spoiled Me Yet"
By Rick Springfield (1949 -)

"So what's it like to die?" I asked, half expecting
him to start laughing.

Coming from any other person, I would have taken
his response as being sarcastic, but sarcasm was not exactly
JP's forte, and his tone was deadly serious, with perhaps a
tinge of loneliness laced into it. "I don't know," he said.
"I've never died."

After weighing his reply, I milked it a bit more by
stating, "But surely you've read up on the subject."

"Yes," came the answer, "But this is one of those
questions that reading up on really doesn't do much good to
answer. It can help formulate your opinions, but the only
way to really know for sure is to die. I *can* tell you that
virtually everyone, regardless of religious belief, race, or
sex, who has ever had a near death experience, has had
similar memories of the experience, namely: passing
through a tunnel of some sort heading towards a light.
Generally, they are at peace and warm, and frequently
accompanied by, or going toward, a loved one."

"So what do you think about that?"

He paused for a moment before he answered. I could
see the wheels churning in his mind.

"Well, science would explain it as the trauma of dying bringing on a vivid reflection of the birth process, which, when you look at it, is actually a pretty good way to think of it, whether there is a life after death or not.

"I often think about what my initial impression will be, assuming my spirit is still alive, when I see my own dead corpse laying there and I fully realize that I'm 'dead'. Will it be panic, fear, shock, relief... what? Apparently, most people's overwhelming impression is one of peace. I guess that comforts me."

All of a sudden, he switched topics. At least I thought he did.

"Let's try an experiment," he said. "I'm going to make a statement, then I'm going to ask you a question. After I ask you the question, I want you to visualize the answer for a moment. Then I'm going to ask you another question. Then we can talk about the results. You ready?"

"Sure," I replied, anxious to see where this was heading.

"Okay," he paused. "You are walking along the beach. What do you see?"

He paused again to let me visualize what I saw. I was about to answer his question when he held up his right hand to stop me from replying. He then asked what I thought was a very interesting follow-up question:

"Do you see yourself?"

I hesitated briefly to picture what I had just frozen in my mind, but the answer came easily: "Yes," I said as I nodded my head.

"That is interesting, and I would have guessed as much," he said.

"Is that supposed to mean something?" I asked.

"According to the article I just finished reading, it suggests that you are more prone to out-of-body experiences than someone who does not visualize themself in their own thoughts. The same can be said for someone who dreams from a birds-eye view, rather than seeing things through their own eyes. I, myself, do not visualize, or dream, from a birds-eye view, I see things from the tip of my nose forward."

"Is there a connection between that and the people who have had near death experiences?" I asked.

"I doubt it; but it's food for thought," he replied. "It just makes you wonder what it is that makes us see things the way we do."

"I'll tell you something that worries me," I said. "I read an article a while back that said a man died at his office and sat there at his desk for two days before someone realized he was dead. People walked by him for *two whole days* before anyone noticed! I can't imagine a more lonely way to go. I guess I don't care so much how I go, so long as someone notices and at least misses me when I do. It just goes to show how meaningless what we do on an everyday basis can be without someone there to share it with you."

"I wish you wouldn't have told me that," he responded. "That is truly a sad story."

We sat for a moment in dulled silence, pondering our inevitable demises. Finally, he put me at ease in more ways than one, mainly, because his statement was statistical, and it appealed to the mathematician in me.

"When you think about how many people die each day, and how few accounts there are of people being revived after being pronounced 'dead' I think there is a reason there are so few accounts."

"And that would be?" I asked.

"Well, we spend our whole lives dodging death, and avoiding it at all costs, but when it boils right down to it, I think there are so few documented cases of near death experiences because people don't *want* to come back. They see the other side and make a conscious decision that whatever it holds is better than what they just left. Even the people who return from beyond have no sense of fear about dying again, and almost every one of them use the same word to describe the 'other side': peace."

"That is true," I noted. "I've never read an account of anyone returning from 'hell'. Now there's a new twist on an old topic."

He chuckled for a moment. "I'll have to look into that."

And once again, we parted ways that night grateful for having shared a half hour of quality time together.

14.
QUESTIONING GOD

"If you have trouble believing in me,
maybe it would help you to know that I believe in you."
- God (George Burns), from the movie Oh, God (1977)

"Not to dwell on the subject," he began the next day, "but I'm interested in this topic of death and the afterlife."

"Knowing a little about your past, I guess I don't blame you," I said.

"Every culture believes in some sort of a God, or Supreme Power. Tied to that Being, whomever or whatever it may be; is generally the belief in some sort of an afterlife. Most people believe that God will reward you in the afterlife if you are 'good', however God defines 'good', in this life. Most people are fairly good people at heart. Thus, it is somewhat safe to assume that most people will be rewarded in the afterlife if, and only if, God exists.

"On the other hand, if God does not exist, I believe it is safe to assume that there is no such thing as an afterlife; that the spirit, or soul, ceases to exist after death; sort of a sleep with no dream. I think this might be the origination of the term 'eternal rest'.

"So, from a non-religious perspective, there are really only two ways to view death. Either:

1) A happier life with God; or
2) An eternal rest: i.e.
annihilation of the soul.

"Either way it doesn't sound too bad, although the latter is infinitely more depressing to think about."

I questioned his logic. "But your assumption that most people are good at heart is a big one. Evil exists, and in some cases, abounds. Thus arises the necessity for a 'hell', or its' equivalent. Assuming, of course, that there is a God."

"True, but if you are basing that statement on the assumption that there is a God, I believe it's safe to assume that a God with the time, talent, and ability to create a system as delicate and precise as ours would not wish the occupants thereof to burn in hell for eternity. However, I will acknowledge that the possibility exists."

"But you're thinking like a Westerner," I stated, recalling former conversations. "Perhaps the possibility exists of a combination of heaven, hell, and annihilation."

I think he could see where I was headed, but he afforded me his respect. "And that would be…"

"Perhaps at death God allows us the privilege of viewing the reward, or punishment, of our life on Earth. We get a glimpse of our own personalized eternity. If we don't like what we see, He shows compassion on us by annihilating us," I surmised.

JP's face was all smiles as he confided, "You learn quickly."

I was on a roll. I'd managed to say something borderline brilliant in two of our last three conversations. I didn't want the moment to end, so I tossed out a question I knew would put him to the test:

"So," I paused for emphasis, "is there a God?"

A deep silence followed as he stared into the distance at the sun setting over Lolo peak. There were several children playing on a trampoline four doors down. The scene was somewhat surreal. It's as if time had stopped and we were the only people on Earth who could move.

He placed the pads of his fingertips over each other and closed his eyes for a moment as if he were in pain. When he opened them again, he looked me straight in the eye and spoke words that to this day still ring in my ears:

"Yes," he said. "There most definitely is a God."

15.
PROVING GOD

"I may be wrong, but I'm not uncertain."
- Glory Road

"You sound convinced," I said. "What makes you so sure?"

A sinister look pierced his brow. "I heard one time that if you took a radio that was in working condition, and took every individual piece out of it, the wires, the speaker, the dials, everything, and put all the pieces in a box and shook it up, then opened the box and flung the pieces into the air, the chances of the pieces falling into place to create the same radio you had just taken apart are greater than the chance of our solar system happening at random."

"I've heard that argument, too," I responded. "But I believe that it's flawed."

"In what way?" he inquired.

"Well, being a computer programmer, I rely on numbers and probability quite extensively, so it's not as if I'm speaking outside of my element. Let's look at the experiment more closely. Would you agree that the pieces of the radio could fall into an infinite amount of configurations, only one of which would form a working radio?" I asked.

"Yes."

"Would you also agree that our universe is infinite?" I asked.

"Yes," he responded again.

"Well then, somewhere in our infinite universe, an infinite number of people are throwing an infinite number of boxes of radio parts into the air. Eventually, one of those infinite numbers of people will have a complete working radio land in front of them; because there exists that one single configuration, and we have an infinite amount of people producing those configurations. Essentially, I've changed the equation from one divided by infinity (one possibility divided by infinite possibilities) to infinity divided by infinity (infinite universe divided by infinite possibilities), or a number divided by itself, which equals one (or 100%). I have now taken your argument and shown that the possibility of our solar system being created by random is 100%."

I grabbed the pen from his shirt pocket and sketched what I was referring to. It looked like this:

If $1/100 + 1/100 + 1/100 + \ldots$ would eventually equal $100/100$, which equals 1.

Then let ∞ = infinity. It would follow that:

$1/\infty + 1/\infty + 1/\infty + \ldots$ would eventually equal ∞/∞, which equals 1.

He examined my equations for a minute, weighing the idea in his mind. I could see the wheels churning. It was quite fascinating watching him 'think'. He then surprised me with his next comment. "I like your concept, but your calculations are flawed."

"How so?" I asked.

"Well, using this same logic, I could guarantee you that if I roll a six-sided dice six times, you will always roll a six at least one of those six times."

He took the pen out of my hand and began jotting down some equations of his own. "Using your logic, the chances of my rolling a six on a six sided dice rolled six times would be diagrammed something like this:"

$1/6 + 1/6 + 1/6 + 1/6 + 1/6 + 1/6 = 6/6 = 1$, or 100%.

I saw immediately that he had a point, which flustered me a bit, because I was a computer science major, and thought my math skills were fairly sound.

He explained further: "When dealing with probability, you need to multiply, not add, and you need to compute the probability that something will *not* happen, and then subtract that percentage from 100 percent."

Again he jotted down a formula, indicative of the correct logic (not the logic I had used):

$$1 - (5/6 * 5/6 * 5/6 * 5/6 * 5/6 * 5/6) =$$
$$1 - (15625/46656) = .6651, \text{ or } 66.51\%.$$

"So, your chances of getting at least one six in six rolls of a six sided dice are 66.51%, not 100%. Here's the formula, ultimately, that you're looking for:"

Let ∞ = infinity (the possibility of the parts landing in any order).

Let T = the number of times you toss the box of radio parts in the air.

Then:

$$\text{Probability of a working radio} = 1 - ((\infty - 1)^T / (\infty^T))$$

I must have looked dazed, because I couldn't, for the life of me, understand how he was deriving these equations so quickly. He must have sensed my frustration, and finally just put it in laymen's terms, so I could understand them, but I still struggled.

"If you just break apart the equation, it makes sense. The numerator (the 'stuff' on top of the division sign), is always growing at a smaller rate than the denominator (the 'stuff' beneath the division sign), because it will always be one less than the denominator, and you're increasing both by the power of the variable 'T'. In essence, the numerator will always get smaller proportionately to the denominator, and a smaller number divided by a bigger number will begin to approach zero the higher that the value of 'T' gets. And then you're subtracting the whole thing from one. So, in a nutshell, the more tries you take, the closer your probability will reach 1 – 0, or 100%."

I chuckled out loud, "You must not sleep very much at night."

A smiled pursed his lips.

Again he glared at his scrawling. He wasn't letting go of this one. Then he added, "But our assumption is that there are an infinite number of people. The argument falls apart if we here on Earth, are the *only* people."

"True, but the same could be said for one person, with an infinite amount of time," I countered, grateful for the opportunity to speak English again.

"Which leads us back to the topic of death," he noted.

I breathed a sigh of relief. There *was* a light at the end of this tunnel. I rushed toward it as fast as I could.

Now, I knew as well as the next guy, maybe even better, that there was no way to prove the existence of God. I believe in God, but I generally enjoy playing the role of Devil's Advocate. This was as good a time as any to do so.

"Surely you weren't basing your knowledge of the existence of God on the radio theory," I scoffed.

"No, no I wasn't," he nodded his head. "There are more decisive ways to prove the existence of God."

"And that would be…" I wondered out loud.

"How much time do you have?" He asked.

"I'd like to know sometime before I die," I said, quite seriously.

"Then allow me to share with you some ideas," he said.

"This'll be good," I thought to myself as I turned the chair around and folded my arms on the backrest, mimicking my mentor.

Then I spoke aloud, "Hit me with your best shot."

16.
IMMORTALITY

"Prepare your mind to receive the best that life has to offer."
- Ernest Holmes (1887 – 1960)

"Before I get started, I want to get your stance on the Bible, and Christianity, in general, although it doesn't necessarily matter. It just makes it a bit easier for me if I know you have a little understanding of either, or both."

What could I say? Religiously speaking, I'm an average Joe who goes to church on Sunday in hopes of scoring some points with The Man Upstairs. Let's just say that if Billy Graham ever came to our town recruiting, I doubt he'd find me a very good candidate.

I answered him as honestly as I knew how.

"Like most Americans, I consider myself a God-fearing man with a fair amount of Biblical knowledge. I am a Christian, but unlike most Christians, I find myself questioning everything, rather than taking things on faith. It's one of my little eccentricities. It drives my wife nuts. It must have something to do with my analytical way of thinking," I said.

"Well, that will probably help you in the long run," he replied. "But we're going to use the Bible as a history book tonight, not necessarily a preaching tool. And I'd be happy to entertain all questions to your liking," he added, as he whipped out a King James version of the Bible that looked like it had never seen a day of rest in it's long life. He shuffled some pages and pointed to an immensely worn out page. "Let's start here, where Jesus is speaking to his apostles:

Luke 9:27 But I tell you
of a truth, there be some
standing here, which shall
not taste of death, till they
see the kingdom of God."

He shuffled back one page. "Now, it's very
important to grasp who Jesus is speaking to here, so let's
turn ahead a couple of verses and find out.

Luke 9:1 Then he called
the twelve disciples
together, and gave them
power and authority over
all devils, and to cure
diseases.

"That verse indicates that Jesus is talking to the
twelve disciples, and here it is reaffirmed to whom he is
speaking:

Luke 9:18 And it came to
pass, as he was alone
praying, his disciples
were with him: and he
asked them, saying,
Whom say the people that
I am?

"If you analyze these three verses together, we have
Jesus speaking to the original twelve apostles and telling
them that there is at least one of them standing there that
will not die until they see the kingdom of God. So now we
need to determine the names of the original twelve apostles.
The best place to find them is in the book of Acts. Keep in
mind that in this verse, Judas, who was called Iscariot, had
already committed suicide, so only the remaining eleven

apostles are named." He flipped the pages again. I counted as he read off the names.

"Acts 1:13 And when
they were come in, they
went into an upper room,
where abode both Peter,
and James, and John, and
Andrew, Philip, and
Thomas, Bartholomew,
and Matthew, James the
son of Alphaeus, and
Simon Zelotes, and Judas
the brother of James.

"Since Judas Iscariot was already dead, Jesus must have been referring to one of these eleven when he said one or more of them would not taste of death until they see the kingdom of God. Now we're going to have to change books for a bit here while we find out how and when the eleven remaining apostles died."

He whisked out a copy of Fox's Book of Martyrs and flipped through the pages in rapid succession, compiling a list of the apostles in the same order as they were mentioned in Acts 1:13.

Peter – Crucified head down in Rome, 66 A.D.
James (son of Zebedee) – beheaded in Jerusalem by Herod (see Acts 12:2)
John – (son of Zebedee) – banished to the Isle of Patmos, 90 A.D. (see Revelations 1:9)
Andrew – Crucified in Edessa, 74 A.D.
Philip – Crucified at Heirapole, Phryga, 54 A.D.
Thomas – Run through by a lance at Corehandal, East Indies, 52 A.D.
Bartholomew – Beaten, crucified and beheaded, 52 A.D.
Matthew – Slain with an axe in Ethiopia, roughly 60 A.D.

James (son of Alphaeus) – Thrown from a pinnacle, then beaten to death, 60 A.D.

Simon Zelotes – Crucified in Presia, 74 A.D.

Judas (the brother of James) – Crucified at Edessa, 72 A.D.

After he had jotted down the final name, he handed me the list and asked simply, "Do you see anything that strikes you as odd?"

I took the paper from him and studied the names carefully.

"There's no date given for James, the son of Zebedee's death," I said.

"True, but his death is one of the two documented by the Bible. Also Herod, better known as Herod Agrippa I, died in 48 A.D.; so those two facts alone solidify James' time of death reasonably well at approximately 48 A.D. What else do you notice?" he asked again.

This time, I studied up and down the list several times. About the third time down the list, the word 'banished' leapt out of the page at me.

"Being banished doesn't necessarily mean John died," I voiced aloud.

"Exactly!" his voice sparked. "But the question that pops out at me is: *why* did they banish him? Why not just kill him like they did all the others?" He paused a moment to let the question sink in. "And the answer to that question is, they *did* try to kill him."

He continued, "John went to Ephesus, a city in Asia Minor, and became the head of the seven churches there. The Emperor at that time, 90 A.D., was a man named Domitian, and he bitterly hated Christians. He ordered a tax upon all Jews, and all who 'lived as Jews', thinking this would include the Christians. But the Christians, who no longer associated themselves with the Jews, refused to pay the tax. This incited Domitian to violence, and because John was their leader, he sent for him to be bound and brought before his council in Rome. There, for all the people to see,

John was thrown into a cauldron of boiling oil. John emerged unscathed. Keep in mind we're talking about a man who's probably at least 75 years old. After what must have been some careful consideration, Domitian decided that if he couldn't kill John, the least he could do would be to get him out of the way; thus the order to banish John to the Isle of Patmos was given, where John remained until Domitian's death in 96 A.D."

Again he pointed at the list of the apostles, and how they'd died.

"So, if you were to choose from this list the one that Jesus was referring to, it would have to be John. Not only is he the only one who didn't die, there's strong evidence that he 'cheated death', actually authenticating Jesus' prophecy."

"But it doesn't stop there," he continued. "Look at this:

> John 21:21 Peter seeing him (the apostle whom Jesus loved, or John) saith to Jesus, Lord, and what shall this man do? John 21:22 Jesus saith unto him, If I will that he tarry till I come, what is that to thee? Follow thou me. John 21:23 Then went this saying abroad among the brethren, that this disciple should not die: yet Jesus said not unto him, He shall not die; but, If I will that he tarry till I come, what is that to thee?"

"That's really ambiguous," I said. "I'm not following it."

"Jesus isn't saying John was not going to die, he's saying he's not going to die *until* Jesus' second coming. The key words are *tarry* and *till*. It seems to me that John, who wrote this passage, is clarifying that the generally accepted fact among the people at the time that he wouldn't die was an incorrect assumption. John knew full well he would die, just not until Jesus returned. He would tarry until then."

"Define tarry for me," I stated, trying to buy time to absorb this evening's material.

He bolted back into his house and was out in an instant with two more books that looked to be frequently used. He cracked opened Webster's II New Riverside Dictionary and quoted:

"Tarry: verb, 1. To delay
or be late in coming or
going: linger. 2. To stay
for a time: sojourn."

He let the dictionary fall from his lap as he hefted Strong's Exhaustive Concordance of the Bible and let me study it:

Tarry: To stay (in a given
place, state, relation, or
expectancy): - abide,
continue, dwell, endure,
be present, remain, stand,
tarry (for), x thine own.

"So what we're talking about here is a man, John, that was promised by Jesus that he would 'tarry', or wait, on Earth, until Jesus' second coming?" I summarized.

"Precisely," he confirmed. "Although, at that time, it was generally considered that Jesus would return again in a short amount of time; fifty years at the most. John probably would have rethought his request if he'd have known it was going to be more than two thousand."

I sat for a moment in numbed silence. He seemed to be content with the silence; too, so we both gazed off into the distance; although I'm sure our minds were in different dimensions. I'd heard of people getting excited about 'discovering' something in the Bible, but this actually *was* exciting.

The hour was getting late. I excused myself after securing the promise that we would continue the topic tomorrow that we'd begun tonight, to which he agreed.

I was getting excited about a religious topic. What next?

17.
THE WAITING

"The most beautiful thing we can experience is the mysterious. It is the source of all true art and science."
- Albert Einstein (1879 – 1955)

The next day began as the previous one had, with JP sitting patiently on his front porch with a veritable library of reference books nestled by his side. Apparently, he didn't feel the need for a recap of yesterday's discussion, because he just dove right in.

"Tonight we're going to switch gears to the twelfth century, roughly 1140 A.D.," he stated. "The Christian movement was about to launch a second crusade against the Muslim armies; in an effort to regain their stronghold of the Holy Land. A letter reportedly began to circulate from a certain man known in the English tongue as Prester John, meaning 'John the Priest', and in the Asian tongue as Wang Kahn: 'The man who wouldn't die'.

"The letter was addressed to the Byzantine Emperor of Rome, Emanuel I, and spoke of a Christian kingdom in 'the East' of which Prester John was ruler. In the letter, the land was reported to have been flowing with milk and honey, and abounding in wealth. The Prester reportedly begged for military help from Emanuel I to protect his people from the barbarians and infidels that were invading his country.

"The first authenticated mention of Prester John was by Otto of Freising, in 1145, who spoke of a king named Prester John who was a descendant of the Magi, and ruled over a fantastically wealthy Christian community in the extreme Orient, beyond the borders of Persia and Armenia.

He had apparently amassed himself a huge army and had already defeated the armies of Media, Persia and Assyria, and was making his way to the Holy Land to crush the Moslems, but was turned back by a rapidly overflowing Tigris river.

"For a long time many Europeans believed that Genghis Khan was, in fact, Prester John. It made sense, since Khan was sweeping central Asia invading Islamic nations in the name of Christianity. The Moslems believed in Prester John, too, and were terrified that someday he would actually return with hordes of armies and crush them.

"In 1177, Pope Alexander III sent his trusted servant Phillipus to Asia to find Prester John. Nothing was ever heard from Phillipus again; but by this time, the rumors had already begun to circulate.

"Suddenly there were myths of Prester John riding into battle on elephants, encountering cannibals, pygmies, horned three-eyed humans, unicorns and phoenixes, all the while maintaining his kingdom, which supposedly housed the Garden of Eden, the Fountain of Youth, the Holy Grail, and fabulous wealth, among other things.

"Hundreds of Christian expeditions were sent to Asia to search for Prester John, but by the end of the fourteenth century, only scant traces of Nestorian Christian communities remained; which redirected the expeditions toward Africa, rather than Asia. This arose from the fact that there was an actual Christian kingdom there, in an area known as Abyssinia, or, what is known as present-day Ethiopia."

"You said Nestorian," I interrupted. "I'm not familiar with that term."

"The Catholic Church, as it stood in the fourteenth century, was a far cry from how the church was originally developed by Jesus 1300 years earlier. 'Nestorian' simply refers to the way the church was initially developed by Jesus himself. You can substitute the word 'traditional' in its place, if you wish."

He continued, "Anyway, the Portuguese sent several expeditions to the Abyssinia kingdom, i.e. Ethiopia, and the reports that were generated confirmed that the kingdom of Prester John had finally been located. As early as 1339 maps were being made that clearly marked the Northeastern section of Africa as the Kingdom of Prester John. These maps continued to be produced until well into the seventeenth century. 'Terra do Preste' it was labeled: 'The land of the Priest'.

"Sir John Mandeville continued the myth in 1366 in his self-titled Travels book, in which he expounded in great detail of the Prester's kingdom. He wrote of 72 provinces, all under the rule of Prester John. He gave a fairly precise description of the land: a rocky ocean to one side, huge unsurpassable mountains on another, and desert in which wild men ran freely on another.

"By the beginning of the fifteenth century, even the Abyssinian priests were beginning to describe their own country as the Kingdom of Prester John. They had, in fact, withstood centuries of attacks by Islam nations, indicating that some Christian forces had indeed been present there.

"So, to summarize, the Europeans, from the eleventh through the sixteenth centuries, believed in a man known as Prester John, a man who ruled a Christian community of great power and wealth. The Prester, to say the least, remained elusive. To the Christians, he was a gift from God. To the Moslems, he represented the possible downfall of their way of life. Although hundreds of letters were forged in the name of Prester John, it is evident that such a man actually did exist. If nothing else, his myth opened up the exploration process to an area that was largely unknown at the time."

He took a long pause and looked at me as if I should be stupefied, which, indeed, I was. I had no clue where he was heading with this.

"So, if I remember correctly, we were discussing the probability that God exists," I stammered. "I'm wondering how this all fits into that…"

"I'm getting to that," he responded. "But, as I said before, this is going to take some time. How 'bout we continue the process tomorrow?" he asked.

"Okay," I said. "But answer me one question first: This Prester John, did he really exist?"

"Like most myths, this one was originally based on fact. Yes, he undoubtedly existed. But as several writers since have put it so eloquently: 'Not a hundredth part of the rumors are true.'"

I basked in the moment briefly, already anticipating tomorrow's discussion, but knowing I had a family at home that needed some fathering.

"See you tomorrow."

"I'll be waiting," he said. "See you then."

18.
LINKS TO THE PRESTER

"It is the mark of an educated mind to be able to entertain a thought without accepting it."

- Aristotle (384 – 322 B.C.)

The following night I drove home from work in a torrential downpour. Northerly winds brought sheets of rain with them as they made their way over Squaw Peak and into the Hub of the Five Valleys. As I pulled into our driveway, I glanced at my mentor who stood on his front porch, undaunted by the weather, awaiting my arrival. As I made a right turn into our garage, I glanced into the rear-view mirror and noticed in awe that he seemed to be standing in his natural element. I hesitated a moment as I reflected on how much this man I knew nothing about had come to mean to me.

I turned off the ignition and made my way into the house to put on some more comfortable clothes and give the wife a peck on the cheek. After a brief moment of complaining to her about how the red tape was growing too thick in my department, I snagged a carrot out of the crisper and told her I'd be back in time for dinner. She, too, was growing accustomed to my extraneous time being spent with my newfound friend. I think she liked the idea, though, because he kept me from spending too much time on the computer. I was also spending a lot of time perusing the Bible these days, and she certainly couldn't find fault with that.

As I stood at the edge of our garage ready to bolt through the downpour to JP's, I looked up for a split second to make sure he was still there. He was. The sheets of rain pelted his head and torso like rocks, but he stood unnerved, almost appearing to enjoy it.

I dashed across the street and up those all too familiar steps. Only then did he break his pose and manage a grin.

"I love this weather," was all he said, although I could barely hear him through the cracking of thunder in the distance.

"Let's go inside today!" I bellowed.

He slung the front door open and I could immediately sense a difference in the décor of his living room. Had it been that long since I'd been in here? The musty smell had been replaced with the inviting smell of cooked food, possibly potatoes. Above the hearth, behind the Ant Farm, he had hung a poster of the sun setting over a vast field of corn. Pastel colors painted the sky from the glowing orange of the sun to shades of purple and auburn that lined the clouds. Printed in light gray letters over the blackish hue of the corn in the foreground were the words:

> "Keep your face to the
> sunshine and you cannot
> see the shadow."
> - Helen Keller (1880 – 1968)

"I like the poster," I said.

"Thanks. Me too," he answered. "Have a seat."

Although he gestured for me to sit on the couch, I chose to sit on the floor due to my soggy clothes. I knew full well he used this couch for his bed, and I wasn't going to provide him with the luxury of an unwanted waterbed for the evening.

"As I recall," he said as he rested on the floor to my right, "we spent the last two evenings discussing history; specifically the history of a certain apostle named John, during the meridian of time, and another man named Prester John, during the middle ages. I don't know if you've made the connection or not, but I want to submit to you that this

Prester John, and John the Beloved Apostle, are one and the same person."

"That seems quite unlikely," I voiced aloud.

"Of course it does, but if you put the pieces together, it fits," he responded. "I'll grant that only a hundredth part of the rumors of Prester John are true, but if you examine the premise of the whole Prester John story, it seems to fit quite nicely with the facts known of the Apostle John.

"Firstly, the fact that Christian nations were found among people who were known to be non-Christian. Somebody had to have been there who knew something about Nestorian Christianity. It wasn't a line of cities, either; it was a spot, seemingly in the middle of nowhere, with no path of Christianity found leading to, or away, from it. It was as if Prester John had a specific place in mind, packed his bags, went directly there, and set up camp.

"Secondly, the fact that the stories began in the middle of the twelfth century, and in the middle of the seventeenth century explorers were still looking for the Prester, some actually having reported to have seen him. If you couple this with the fact that to the Asian people he was known as 'the man who wouldn't die' it seems likely that perhaps he was the one who was told he would tarry until Jesus came again. There can't be that many people in the world with 500-year life spans.

"I didn't mention it the day before yesterday, but all the Apostles, including John, were given a charge by Jesus to 'Go ye therefore, and teach all nations...' so John must have felt some obligation to preach in distant lands, as Jesus had instructed him to do."

"It just seems kind of weak to me," I said. "Isn't there some kind of link between Prester John and John the Apostle during the 1000 years or so between the two time periods?"

"None that I'm aware of," he said. "And believe me I've tried to find it. It just doesn't seem to exist."

"So, let's assume you are correct about Prester John and John the Apostle being the same person. What does that mean?" I inquired.

"Well, if you'll remember correctly, this whole ordeal started with our discussion regarding the existence of God."

His eyes twinkled a bit as he continued, "This means that there is a God," he paused for emphasis. "Would you not agree that mankind, in general, has a mortality rate of less than one hundred years?"

"Yes."

"Then how can you ignore the possibility of anything but God allowing a man to live for 1700 years without dying?"

"I don't know," I said slowly. And then in my typical antagonistic way, I added, "Maybe there is such a thing as the fountain of youth, and maybe Prester John did locate it."

"And he just happened to be Nestorian Christian and happened to have the same name as the Apostle that had been granted the gift of immortality one thousand years earlier?" he balked. "Even if Prester John *had* discovered the fountain of youth, the similarities are just too strong to be a coincidence. I'm not sure the existence of a fountain of youth, if there is one, isn't proof of God in and of itself. Science sure wouldn't be able to explain it."

"You have a point," I conceded. "Any record of Prester John ever dying?"

"There's really no record that he was ever even found at all, dead or alive."

"Then why are you putting so much stock in this story?" I begged.

He paused for a long moment. He glanced up at me several times as if he was trying to weigh my mind. Finally, he sighed and said, "There's another scripture that I'd like you to look at when you get some time tonight. Sleep on it. We can talk about it tomorrow."

He scribbled on a piece of paper and placed it in my hand as he walked me to the door. The rain was letting up and the clouds were starting to dissipate over the Western sky, allowing shards of sunlight to illuminate the valley. I glanced down at the note in my hand and then back again to his weathered face. He was drinking in the scene.

"I'll see you tomorrow," I said.

"I'll be waiting," he answered.

I sauntered across the street a little more slowly than I had when I approached, undaunted by the drizzle that had previously been a downpour. As I closed the garage door behind me, he was still on his porch looking up at the sky.

I pulled the Bible from off of our living room bookshelf and sat down at the coffee table to read the verse he had given me. I read it about four times, each of which had a different meaning to me. I wasn't sure what he was trying to indicate, but no matter how I read it, it left me terribly confused:

> Revelation 1:9: I John, who also am your brother, and companion in tribulation, and in the kingdom and patience of Jesus Christ, was in the isle that is called Patmos, for the word of God, and for the testimony of Jesus Christ.

19.
HE'S STILL ALIVE

"The beginning of knowledge is the discovery of something
we do not understand."

- Frank Herbert (1920 – 1986)

In the Northeast corner of Missoula, about as far
from my home as you can get and still be in Missoula,
where Rattlesnake Creek empties into the Clark Fork River,
lies Hellgate Canyon. Hellgate Canyon derived its' name in
the 1800's, because settlers traveling west used to arrive in
the Missoula Valley through the canyon, and they would
frequently be ambushed by Indians awaiting their arrival.
The Indians would wait atop the jagged cliffs that lined both
sides of the Clark Fork. Trapped between the walls of the
Canyon and the River, the settlers had no chance of
escaping an ambush. The Indians knew what they were
doing. What started out being called Hell's Gate eventually
ended up as Hellgate. The name fit, and stuck.

Today, however, the area had been set aside as one
of the most wonderful parks I'd ever seen: Greenough Park.
Etched into the Canyon alongside Rattlesnake Creek, the
grass seemed to go on forever. There were bicycle trails
leading off into the mountains, lots of park benches, and
best of all, the thundering of water could be heard as the
Creek hit the River. Greenough Park was everything a Park
should be, and then some.

I'd discovered six years ago that taking the extra
hour to cross town was well worth the effort, and tonight
was the perfect night to do it. So we threw some chicken
and Oreos and soda in a cooler and all piled in the Caravan.
The kids were almost as excited as their Dad.

There has always been something very rewarding
about looking at my kids in the rear-view mirror. It might

have something to do with the fact that that's the only time when I can look them in the eye, and measure their growth. If I adjust the mirror just right, I can usually catch all of them at the same time; Nathan and Vanessa toward the front, Valerie in the middle of the back seat. If I steer with my left hand, I can hold Gwen's hand with my right, it has a way of pulling the whole family together; makes me feel important.

As the kids bailed out of the car, I reminded them to stay together, and not go too far. Gwen added that they needed to stay within earshot, so they could hear us when we called them for dinner.

Valerie headed off toward the swings, while Vanessa and Nathan headed for the creek: so much for staying together. Gwen and I sat down on our favorite bench and watched the kids while we listened to the gushing of the water.

A few moments later, Nathan returned holding a three-foot long aspen branch and asked if he could use it to catch fish. When I asked him how he planned on doing that, he explained that if he drug the branch on top of the water, a hungry fish would come along and latch on to one of the leaves. All he'd have to do then is pull the branch out of the water, and he'd have himself a fish.

I asked him what kind of fish he planned on catching. I thought his answer suggested quite a bit of foresight for a ten-year old.

He grinned as he responded, "Stupid ones."

Gwen and I got a good chuckle out of that, but I gave him my blessing and wished him good luck. He scurried off in the direction of the 'stupid fish'.

The evening went by quickly. We ate at various times because we all had something going on at one time or another, and it wasn't like we had to be together to munch on a piece of chicken.

Vanessa and Gwen and I sat for quite a while with our shoes off, dipping our feet into the creek. The water was icy-cold, but it felt good in contrast to the warm weather. Vanessa has a way of being quiet, and then suddenly breaking in to a cat-that-ate-the-canary grin. Gwen and I think she has a sweetheart, but she never confesses it if she does. I don't exactly discourage it if she does, it just makes me feel old knowing my twelve year old is developing feelings for the opposite sex. I know I sure did when I was twelve.

As we sat along the rocks lining the creek, Nathan came rushing back and proclaimed, "Dad, come here, quick!"

He informed us that he had found something cool. I yanked on my shoes and hustled along, trying to catch up to him as he made his way northward along the creek. After chasing him for about forty yards, he veered to the left, away from the creek for about ten feet. By the time I reached him, he was standing on the branch he'd been using as his fishing pole, pointing the index finger of his right hand down toward the ground.

"Look!" was all he said.

I followed his finger and saw immediately what he was so excited about. A channel of the creek had dried up, and in its lethal embrace was a four-inch speckled cutthroat trout, trying to retrieve what little oxygen it could from the rapidly diminishing pool of water. The pool was so shallow that the dorsal fin of the trout was protruding above the water. In another twenty-four hours, this fish would have been history.

"Did you try to catch it with your pole?" I asked.

"Yeah, but I think all it did was make him mad," he replied.

About this time, Vanessa crept up behind us to see what was going on. She saw the stranded fish and asked, "Is he still alive?"

I hesitated for a moment before I answered. There was something in her question that held a certain 'applicability' to other events that had been transpiring in my life. I pondered the question again before I answered.

"He won't be for long, unless we save it," I responded, and then added, "but yes, he is still alive."

"Let's kill it," Nathan said, in typical ten-year old fashion.

"No," Vanessa whined. "Help it."

"Can we keep it?" Valerie asked, who had now joined in the spectacle.

"I'm with Vanessa," I said. "I think we should save it."

Nathan bowed his head in obvious displeasure that we were going to let such a fine prize get away from our dinner table. But after I told him that one fish stick couldn't feed five people, he seemed to come around. Logic works well with kids, sometimes.

I kicked off my shoes and socks and sauntered out into the pool. It was about twenty degrees warmer than the main body of the creek. I arched my back over the frightened fish. While cupping its' spine with my left hand, I slowly scooped under its' jaw with my right, and gently applied more pressure until I had a firm grip. With what remaining fight it had, it squirmed to try to get away. I wondered, if he knew what I was trying to do, would he squirm so much?

I made a hasty retreat to the main body of the creek as the weathered rocks stung the pads of my feet. Once again I bent over, this time to release my catch. The icy water lapped at my ankles as I slowly lowered the cutthroat into it. I wiggled my hands back and forth for just a moment before letting go, to get the little guy use to the water. And then I slowly released him.

The girls seemed to take it a little better than Nathan did, but I think Nathan eventually saw the wisdom of the whole event. He was just glad he'd seen a fish up close.

On the way home, Valerie wanted to know why we didn't keep it. It's more difficult than it sounds to explain to a six year old why a four-inch trout won't stay alive for very long in a six-inch fishbowl. Gwen finally calmed her by telling her that we'd come back some other time and try and find its' babies. That seemed to do the trick.

With the smell of fresh fish still pungent on my hands, I made the last turn down the cul-de-sac to our home. I was suddenly overcome by an overwhelming thought. As I approached our driveway, I craned my neck to the left to see if JP was on his porch. To my elation, he was. I slowed to a halt and rolled down the window. Straining my neck outside of the car, I yelled in JP's direction, "You think he's still alive, don't you?"

He looked up from his book and studied me for a brief moment. An intriguing look enveloped his face. Yelling wasn't his style, so he just smiled and gave me a thumbs up.

I pondered the reaction a moment before continuing on. As I was about to gun the gas, another thought occurred to me.

Again, I craned my neck out the window and yelled, "You know who he is, don't you?"

Once again, he nodded his head in the affirmative and gave me a thumbs up.

"I'll see you tomorrow," I finally yelled.

And yet again, another nod, and another thumbs up.

I pulled in to our garage and instructed the kids to go get their pajamas on and brush their teeth. Gwen gave me a quizzical look and asked, "Who is 'he'?"

I wasn't quite sure how to respond, so I just said that JP was studying a mystery man in the Bible. She didn't pursue it, and I was grateful.

I was feeling pretty good about myself, having spent some quality time with the family, so I hit the hay with a clear conscience. As I reached over on the nightstand to douse the light, I noticed the Bible laying open to the verse I had pondered earlier that evening. I read it again.

Revelation 1:9: I John, who also am your brother, and companion in tribulation, and in the kingdom and patience of Jesus Christ, was in the isle that is called Patmos, for the word of God, and for the testimony of Jesus Christ.

This time, his meaning seemed a little clearer.

20.
IDENTIFYING THE BODY

"If I were two-faced, would I be wearing this one?"
- Abraham Lincoln (1809 – 1865)

The next day at work drug on forever. I checked the clock about every ten minutes throughout the course of the whole morning. By the time lunch came around, I was a mess. I decided to take the rest of the day off. I could use the time off, anyway. The last time I'd taken a vacation was in February, for a friend of my wife's wedding. Other than that, I had about 112 hours left to use, and the company's policy on vacation time was 'use it or lose it'. I definitely didn't want to lose it. It was Friday anyway; nobody else was getting anything done. Why should I?

I gave Gwen a call to let her know I'd be home for lunch and ask her if she needed me to pick anything up at the store on the way home. She couldn't think of anything. I gave the avocado plants on my desk a thorough watering and told them to have a nice weekend. I've never been able to grow anything, but for some reason my thumbs turn green when I pick up an avocado pit. From what I've read on the Internet, if I can keep it up for nine more years, I'll have an avocado for lunch everyday. Somehow I don't think my boss will take too kindly to having two ten foot avocado trees in my cube, though.

I took the back route home. The sun was full and there was a mild breeze; enough to convince me to keep the window down instead of using the air conditioner. Taking Highway 93 at noon through Malfunction Junction on a Friday is generally not a good idea, and although the back roads take about twice as long, they looked a little friendlier to me today than usual. I can usually spot a hawk or two if I look close enough. I didn't see any, but I did spot three or four unfortunate rabbits, (or were they cats?), that had become a permanent part of the road.

Turning on to our street I was surprised to see that JP was sitting on his front porch, feet kicked up, taking it all in. It seemed like every time I came home, no matter what time it was, he was there. It was noon for crying out loud; didn't he do anything for a living?

I slowed the car before turning into our driveway and poked my head out the window, "Must be nice," I said, "not having to work for a living."

A big grin spread across his face and he held up a book. "I am working," he said.

"You got time to talk?" I asked.

"Always," he replied.

"Let me get a bite to eat and I'll be over in a second," I said, then punched the gas and pulled in to our garage.

Gwen cooked grilled tuna and cheese sandwiches. All three kids were parked at the table wolfing them down. I grabbed one while there was still one left to grab.

"You're home early," she said.

"Some days I just can't stand being at work. I was gonna mow the lawn, but I think I'll go over and talk to JP instead. I'll get to the lawn later tonight when it's cooler."

"You're spending an awful lot of time over there," she noted. "Does he mind?"

"It's kind of odd, but I think he loves it. I'm pretty sure he's lonely," I responded with my mouth full of tuna. "He's out there waiting every time I come home. Do you ever see him go anywhere?"

"No," she said. "But I haven't really been taking notes."

"He just seems kind of lonely, and I think he likes the company," I said.

So I gulped the last swallow of milk and gave Gwen another peck on the cheek and I was out the door. "Thanks for lunch," I said. She responded, but I didn't catch what it was, I was in too much of a hurry to get to JP's.

He didn't even wait 'til I was seated to ask how I'd slept. My foot was on his bottom stair and he just blurted it out, "Bet you didn't sleep very well."

"No, as a matter of fact I didn't," I admitted.

"Did you look at the homework I gave you?" he asked.

"I did, but I really didn't know what to think. I wasn't sure what you meant by it."

"Hmmm," he mused. "Perhaps I chose poorly. Maybe if I gave you a little clearer verse. Try this one."

He flung open the Bible and indicated with his index finger which one he wanted me to read. It was short:

> John 4:26: Jesus saith
> unto her, I that speak unto
> thee am he.

There went my misunderstanding. It all of a sudden became very clear that what I had thought he meant, was indeed what he meant.

The silence was awkward. I sat wondering what to say; while he sat waiting for me to voice my opinion. He could sense how I was feeling though, and finally he was the one who broke the silence.

"Bryce, there's really no other way to tell you this, but I am John the Apostle. I am Prester John."

"So you're telling me you're approaching two thousand years old?" I laughed.

"One thousand, nine hundred and seventy eight, to be exact," he said, somewhat annoyed at my joviality.

"Be real," I muttered, concerned with his seriousness. "Have you seen a doctor?"

"There's no need to see a doctor, because whether you believe me or not, does not change the fact that I am who I say I am."

I was getting frustrated. "So I have a two thousand year old man living across the street from me?" I mocked. "And why does a two thousand year old man choose to spend his time on a front porch in Missoula Montana talking to a hack computer programmer about nothing in particular? You don't need me, you need someone who can help you."

"Maybe that's why I'm here, Bryce. Maybe you're the one who can help me."

"And how could I do that?"

"Well, you can start by believing me."

"Sorry. I don't see that happening."

"Then let's go back to our conversation about the radio parts. There was one chance in an infinite amount of possibilities that the radio could fall together in working order. By your own admission, the very fact that that one possibility exists proves that it *can* happen, no matter how remote the possibility."

"And you're saying it's happening to me?" I chided.

"Yes," he answered confidently.

"Why me?" I asked again.

"It's like I said, maybe you are the one who can help me."

"What do you want me to do?"

"You're doing it," he said, to my surprise.

"What? Sitting here on your front porch night after night talking about hypothetical situations and yapping about nothing in particular? I don't see that as being much of a help to a man who claims he's Jesus' right hand man."

He was hurt. "I wouldn't consider our conversations yapping. Some of the finest conversations I've ever had have been with you."

"You're telling me you've been taught by Jesus and reigned for 1500 years as a King, and yet some of the best discussions you've ever had have been with me? And why is that?"

"I think you underestimate daily life, Bryce. It isn't necessarily the highlights that carry us through the day-to-day grind, it's the people we associate with every day that make or break us. If we find a 'niche' that we enjoy, and keep hold of for a while, it makes life that much more tolerable. You're logical. You weigh the facts. You're open-minded. You think before you react. The bottom line is that I enjoy talking to you."

He continued: "Do you think there's any way I would have told you this if I didn't think you'd believe me? I've gone to great lengths to avoid being labeled insane by everyone I've ever met. You try remaining anonymous for 1900 years. Try it for a year. It's extremely difficult to forever stay in hiding. Human nature, by nature, longs for company. You've got to tell someone, and I told you because I believed in you. And I still do."

"And your telling me makes you somehow feel better?"

"When you come to believe what I'm saying is true; yes, it does."

"And what happens if what I come to believe is exactly what I believe now?"

"Then I will have failed," he said.

"Failed what?" I asked.

"What I've come here to do," he responded quietly.

21.
RE-EXPLAINING

"I hope I will be able to confide everything in you, as I have never been able to confide in anyone, and I hope you will be a great source of comfort and support."
                                        - Anne Frank (1929 – 1945)

"Allow me to back up and start at the beginning," he said.

"Please do," I responded, irritated at his premise, but knowing the least I could do for him was hear him out.

"I was born the second son to Zebedee and Salome on what would correspond with our current calendar date of June 12, 13 A.D. My older brother's name was James. His birth date would correspond with our current calendar date of March 21, 9 A.D. We were raised in the city of Capernaum on the banks of the Sea of Galilee. My father was quite wealthy and owned a fishing company with five men working for him, in addition to my brother and myself.

"At the age of seventeen, as my brother and I were helping our father mend his fishing nets, we were approached by a man the likes of which we had never met. He was a simple man, yet he spoke as though he knew the answers to all of life's questions. There was something magnetic about him, and he asked my brother and I to come with him. My father must have sensed that whatever this man had to offer was worthwhile, because James and I both looked at him and he nodded his approval without uttering a word. There were neither tears nor hugs, just simple understanding, as we said our goodbyes.

"The relationship grew as we spent the days together. My brother and I were labeled 'Boangeres', meaning 'Sons of Thunder', because of our feistiness and bull-headedness. I believe I was a little more in tune than the other eleven who chose to follow, and I became best friends with the man known today as Jesus of Nazareth.

"For three years we followed him, listening and trying to understand. He spoke differently than everyone else, in so many ways more plainly, yet what he said was never received the same way by any two people. I guess that's part of what made him so captivating, so magnetic.

"At one point, my brother and I requested of him that he grant us whatever we desired, to which he consented. We asked that when we arrived in heaven, we be given the honor of sitting one on his right hand, and one on his left hand. If it was his to give, I'm sure he would have granted it to us; but it was not his to give. I later made a similar request to dwell on the earth until his second coming. More specifically, my request was that I would not die until he came again. This time, he granted my request."

"Did he grant anyone else that request?" I asked.

"Not for immortality," he replied. "But all of the Apostles were granted a wish of some sort, the bulk of which came in the form of Jesus speedily remembering them when they enter heaven, upon their deaths." Then he added, quite sadly, "They chose wisely."

He continued. "Many people have asked the question why I, John, was the only one of the twelve to stand with Jesus at his crucifixion. I'm certain that the other eleven, save Judas, would have gladly stood by his side were it not for the Roman's thirst for blood. The answer is twofold:

1) Because I was his best
friend, and
2) I did not fear the
Romans; because I knew
that Jesus' promise to me
was valid, and they could
not kill me.

"As I stood at his feet and ripped at my skin for what
they were doing to my best friend, he asked of me a favor.
He asked me to behold his mother. In doing so, he was
asking me, his best friend, to ensure that his mother would
be taken care of. It was an honor to be able to show him
what insignificant amount of support that I could, and I
nodded in agreement. He actually smiled at me from the
cross as I did." He stopped and repeated himself; "He
smiled at me through his pain."

"Is the Biblical account of the crucifixion accurate,
then?" I asked.

"Yes," he replied. "But you can't even begin to get a
sense of the anguish and intensity of the moment unless you
were there. I think the word 'Passion' is a fairly accurate
one-word depiction of the whole ordeal."

He paused for a minute, and then continued. "I spent
the next thirty years tending to the needs of a woman who
had witnessed her son cruelly tortured before her eyes. She
took it as well as a mother possibly could, but she had some
very bad days. There was almost as much honor in her eyes
as she lay dying in my arms as there was in her sons' thirty
years previous. She was a valiant woman.

"I began preaching immediately after her death, with
some degree of success, until opposition became so strong
that people were literally hiding from the Christian
movement for fear of their lives should they be 'discovered'
by the government to be a 'Christian'. Then Domitian took
the governmental seat and began slaughtering everyone

professing to be Christian. I was one of the primary Christians whom he tried to remove. The story I told you before about the boiling oil was true. I didn't feel a thing. He figured it would serve his purpose to simply exile me, so that's what he did.

"I remained on the Isle of Patmos for almost seven years, wherein I had the Revelation of the course of events for the rest of time, as we understand time. The very same course of events through which I now knew I would have to patiently endure, no matter how long it took. It was that Revelation that truly changed my heart to become the man I believe Jesus saw in me the day he beckoned me to follow him.

"After Domitian's death in 96 A.D., nobody knew what to do with me. Eventually, the guards simply unlocked my chains and told me I was free to leave. I had nowhere to go. I returned to Capernaum for a short time, but my friends and family were all dead. There was nothing there for me. It was then that I fully realized the course that I had chosen for myself. Feeling very alone, and somewhat scared, I picked up pen and ink and began to write. I wrote of the relationship that I had had with the greatest man the world will ever know. I wrote of his love and compassion for everyone. My writings were later translated and compiled into the book we now know as The Gospel of St. John.

"On the one hand, I had been commissioned by Jesus to preach the gospel. On the other, there was a radical movement going on in my homeland to eliminate my people. I'd had enough of a life in exile, so I made the decision to go to a country in which I would be welcomed, and in which my thoughts would not forever dwell on the absence of friends and loved ones. I began a very slow trek toward a land now known as India; but back then was simply known to Europeans as 'the East'. I began the second phase of my perpetual existence; an existence in which I would come to be known as Prester John.

"But I've talked your ear off enough for tonight. I'll continue tomorrow, if you'll let me."

I welcomed the break. I couldn't believe he was serious. "I'll see you tomorrow then," I said.

"I'll be waiting," he answered.

22.
OFF HIS ROCKER

"Truly great madness cannot be achieved
without significant intelligence."
- Henrik Tikkanen (1924 – 1984)

From everything I'd ever witnessed about JP, he had
the sharpest mind I'd ever known. I wondered if it was
possible to have the sharpest mind I'd ever witnessed, while
at the same time not be in his right mind. I'd heard about
Van Gogh and Beethoven being a bit on the eccentric side,
possibly even insane, but I'd never heard of a genius that
had multiple personalities.

Trying to sleep was useless. All I was managing to
do was annoy my wife with my tossing and turning. At best,
I'm generally not a sound sleeper, but tonight was beyond
that. Finally, at about 1:30, I swaggered out of bed and went
to the front room to stare across the street at what I once
again deemed to be my psychotic neighbor's house. The
lights were out and the wet driveway glistened with the
orange glow of the street lamp. I stood there for a long while
hoping some revelation would come to me; but it didn't.
After what seemed to be about ten minutes, I turned and
started toward the kitchen to get some milk. The bookshelf
caught my eye and, out of curiosity, I pulled down the
dictionary.

> Schizophrenia: noun. A
> mental disorder marked
> by loss of awareness of
> reality, often with
> disturbances of behavior
> and the inability to
> reason.

That didn't describe JP at all; not even the 'awareness of reality' part. He was more aware of his surroundings than anybody I'd ever met. The 'inability to reason' part was way off base, too. There must be some other term to describe what he was suffering from. The only word I could conjure up was 'loony'. Was that a medical term?

After chugging some milk directly from the carton, which my wife hates but I do anyway, I made my way to the basement and logged on to the Internet to do some research. I typed in 'multiple personalities' and ran a scan. 94 hits. Most of the pages addressed the combination of multiple personalities and Dissociative Identity Disorders (DIDs), which, as far as I could tell, are fairly commonly diagnosed in adults that have suffered varying degrees of child abuse.

But what I read didn't fit, either. The cases that were discussed were almost exclusively where a person 'pops' into another personality to accommodate (or protect themselves from) their immediate surroundings. As far as I could gather, it was a self-induced defense mechanism to protect an individual from a given situation. JP had indicated that he hadn't stayed in one place for very long, so I didn't automatically dismiss the concept, but at the same time it just didn't feel right.

After sufficiently convincing myself that I was not good at diagnosing mental disorders, I began wondering what, if anything, I could do to help JP. This had to be some kind of a bad joke, there's no way he could be serious. But JP wasn't exactly the prankster type. Man, maybe it was me that was out of my mind. Pull yourself together, Bryce.

Somewhere around 3:30, I decided the best thing for me to do was to do nothing. I liked JP. I had spent about half an hour every day for the last month with him and I didn't want that to change. At the very worst, he was asking me to help him, and I was more than happy to do that if that's what he needed.

Out of respect for my wife, I yanked a pillow and blanket down from the top shelf of the closet and spent the remainder of the evening on the couch in the living room. I'd get a better view of reality tomorrow.

23.
OUT OF AFRICA

Yesterday upon the stair,
I met a man who wasn't there.
He wasn't there again today.
I wish that man would go away.
   - Hughes Mearns (1875 – 1965)

I had mixed emotions as I made my way over to his house the next afternoon. On the one hand, I was learning a lot about history, and it was quite interesting. On the other, I couldn't help but feel that I was hearing it from a man who wasn't quite right upstairs. But then again, I felt the least I could do was hear him out. I helped him recall where he was.

"Yesterday, I believe you left off with the beginning of Prester John's life."

He nodded in agreement, and picked up right where he'd left off.

"I took my time as I headed east. I made my way through what is now Turkey, Iraq, Iran, and portions of Southern Asia, Afghanistan, and Pakistan. Finally I established what I called 'home' in India. I was pleasantly surprised by how many people I came across who were familiar with the Christian movement, and I met several groups of people who had been visited by the apostles Thomas and Matthew. They had done their job well.

"Although I believe the people meant well, it was apparent that what they had been taught fifty years earlier had, to a large degree, been unrecognizably distorted, and I spent several years in remote villages putting forth a great deal of effort to get the people back on track.

"You asked me before why there isn't some sort of record linking John the Apostle to Prester John. I suppose the main reason is that I didn't stay put long enough for anyone to feel I was significant enough to write about. The connection between the Apostle and the Prester had not yet been made.

"People have a tendency to treat you strangely when they grow from infancy to adulthood, and you haven't aged a bit. For that reason, I made a habit of moving roughly every ten years. You wouldn't believe how many times I've had someone tell me: 'You remind me of someone I used to know' – when, in reality, I *was* that person they used to know. I learned quickly that for my own protection it was best to remain silent and elusive.

"I headed north, around 800 A.D., mainly because the people there were very receptive to Christianity, and I was far enough east to be out of harms' way. I spent the next 300 years at the western edge of the Gobi desert teaching and establishing the Church in cities named Bishbaligh, Almalyk, Kashgar, Khotan and Yarkand. To the Chinese, I was in the West; to the Europeans, I was in the East. It was the perfect no man's land for which I had been seeking.

"The area became known as the Five Cities region; the crossroads of the East and the West. Sir John Mandeville described it quite accurately when he said it was nearly inaccessible. We had the Altay Mountains to the east of us, which bordered the Gobi desert on the west, and to the south of us we had the Taklimakan Desert and beyond that, the nearly impenetrable Himalayan Mountains.

"I enjoyed my stay there. It was peaceful and the people revered me as their king, although I preferred to be called their leader. I watched six generations come and go. I loved the people, and they loved me. We thrived for most of those 300 years. I became known as Prester John: 'the man who wouldn't die.'

"Then, in 1095 A.D., word spread of the Crusades, the 'Christian' effort to re-take the Holy Land from the Muslims. Apparently, the Holy Land was not big enough for the Christians, and the movement began migrating east.

"By the mid twelfth century, word had spread of the Five Cities area, and that it was ruled by a Christian man. Emanuel I, the Byzantine Emperor of Rome, forged a letter, in my name, to persuade the people of Rome that the Crusades should be directed to 'the East', in an effort to aid me in defending Christianity. Nothing could have been further from the truth. I was enjoying the peaceable kingdom of the Five Cities, and from what I had heard, Christianity had become so distorted that I didn't want to be a part of what it had become.

"A defense system suddenly became necessary, and the next few years were set aside to educate the Five Cities region in the art of war, and how to defend themselves. Rumors began that we were 'marching through the heart of China' on our way to the Holy Land, but that too, could not have been further from the truth. We stayed put, and valued the freedom we had in our own land. We didn't need any more land, nor did we want it."

I interrupted, "So you became a warrior?"

"'Warrior' is a little too strong of a term, and not me, specifically. I'm not much of a fighter," he replied. "We never did take the offensive, we were there to defend, not invade."

He continued, "Due to the treacherous climate to our west, we were able to defend ourselves successfully for the next fifty years. By the time enemy armies reached our land, they were so depleted from the travel that they were lacking in numbers and strength. Those whom we didn't convert, we simply turned back. Very few, if any, were killed. I made sure of that.

"By the beginning of the thirteenth century, I had heard rumors of a man named Genghis Khan from Mongolia who was an incredibly successful military leader, and word spread that he was marching west to conquer us. It was obvious to me that if I were to do nothing, the people of the Five Cities would either be crushed by Genghis Khan from the east, or slaughtered by the Crusades from the west. In

1219 A.D., I took the initiative and said my final goodbye's to the people of the Five Cities, and set out to meet Genghis Khan in Karakorum, his capital city."

"So you're telling me you knew Genghis Khan?" I questioned.

His answer was interesting, and made me question myself. He chuckled and asked me, in reply, "I told you yesterday that I knew Jesus personally, and you're questioning the fact that I knew Genghis Khan? That seems a bit backward.

"But to answer your question, yes, I did know Genghis Khan. He was certainly not the barbaric person that I had prepared myself to meet. I found him to be most pleasant, and almost converted him. We became very good friends. As a result of our friendship, he ensured me that he would spare the Five Cities, and concentrate his armies to the West. He was true to his word. He actually far surpassed his word by taking the offensive and marching his troops as far west as Iraq, sparing the Nestorian Christians as he went. You can bet the Catholics in Rome were very nervous as Khan approached the Holy Land; but he stopped short, much to their relief.

"Once again, the relationship we cultivated spawned rumors that were simply not true; the most interesting of which spoke of us being brothers, and offering women to each other as wives. These were both unfounded. At any rate, I added another nickname to my ever-increasing repertoire: Wang Khan.

"From Karakorum I made my way south to the Gulf of Cambay on the mid-western coast of India. I stayed there for three years, until I was certain the Five Cities area would be spared. I then boarded a ship and sailed west-southwest across the Arabian Sea to the Gulf of Aden, which juts into the Eastern coast of Africa. The rumors of treacherous seas were true. Our ship capsized after colliding with an uninhabited rocky island during a severe storm. For the second time in my rather lengthy life, I tested my immortality by treading water for four days. Eventually, the torrential currents carried me to the Eastern banks of Ethiopia, known then as Abyssinia, to a city known today as Djibouti.

"My life in Abyssinia wasn't altogether different than it was in the Five Cities region. Scant remnants of Matthew's work remained, and the people were quite receptive to rekindle the Nestorian effort. The Abyssinian region was overwhelmed with natural resources, namely gold, diamonds and emeralds, which made for easy trade with neighboring countries. Once the people were unified, the whole country prospered. And once again, I was chosen to be their leader.

"I never felt as naturally protected by the Abyssinian land as I had in the Five Cities region, however. Explorers were constantly emerging from the west seeking the kingdom of Prester John. It became particularly bad when, toward the middle of the fifteenth century, all the efforts to seek me in Asia had been abandoned; and Northern Africa became the target of their searches. I thwarted this for about three hundred years by simply living in people's homes. I moved from city to city, home to home, with no definite plan of where I would go next. I simply asked the people not to give too many specifics on my whereabouts, should any foreigners come looking for me. This allowed them to answer honestly when they replied that I had passed through but weren't sure where I was headed.

"Eventually, I grew weary of hiding, and decided I needed to regain my anonymity. One evening, I simply started walking south along the Eastern coastline of Africa. For several months I didn't really even speak to anyone. It was a lonely time, seeing as I had just spent the previous 1600 years preaching and leading people. It was the first time I could ever recall my life actually being quiet, and to my amazement, I enjoyed it.

"Sleeping on the rocky shores of Eastern Africa, I made my way south through Kenya and Tanzania until I reached Mozambique. I boarded a ship and crossed the Mozambique Channel to the Island of Madagascar. I allowed myself the luxury of settling down and enjoying life for a while. It was relatively quiet, and I loved the land. I spent several years there employed by a man named Mahmud, who had migrated from India and had purchased land to farm rice."

His mood changed, quite drastically, from spirited to great soberness. Up to this point, I'd gotten the feeling that he was simply stating history. But it suddenly got very personal.

"It was while I was in Mahmud's employ that I met his daughter Sarala. By all counts she was a common woman, but to me she was beautiful. Her mind was as keen a mind as I had ever come across. We would sit for hours looking out across the Indian Ocean discussing topics that fascinated us. We would gaze at each other like any two people falling in love might do, much like how you and your wife were looking at each other at the party the other night. I was going to ask her father for her hand in marriage, but Sarala contracted typhoid fever before I ever got the chance. The typhoid gave way to pneumonia, and before I knew it, she had passed on. There was nothing I could do but watch her die.

"This might sound odd, but it was the first time in my life that I viewed my immortality as a curse, rather than a blessing. I sat for days by her side looking at her empty frail body and wishing I could join her. A large portion of myself was buried when she was. For the first time in my life, I longed to die.

"I had withstood centuries of watching as my family, friends, and peers passed from this world, but this one hurt the most. I suddenly felt very alone. Half the Eastern Hemisphere revered my name, yet I had no true friends. I had the sudden realization that whatever true friends I would develop, would pass this same course, and I would be forced to stand by and rejoice for them in their passing, all the while aching that it would never be me."

He waited for a moment in silence, and then snapped back into story-telling mode.

"Once again I migrated to the African mainland and made my way north. The further north I traveled, the more I became aware that times were changing, and, although men were mostly barbaric in their actions, new ideas were cropping up that kept me fascinated. I heard of a man named Nicolaus Copernicus from Poland who was bold enough to openly theorize that the sun was the center of our solar system, and that the earth spins on its axis daily, and once yearly around the sun. I heard of a man named Galileo Galilei from Italy that built powerful instruments to look at the heavens, and that he had actually verified the authenticity of Copernicus' work.

"Although both these men were criticized for openly rebelling against the Roman Catholic Church, and labeled heretics by those who would only accept the 'Earth-based' solar system philosophy, their ideas started people thinking for themselves, and reasoning, rather than fighting. It also brought to light to the general public the idea that perhaps the Roman Catholic Church wasn't all that it was held up to be.

"Shortly thereafter a man named Isaac Newton of Great Britain put forth some groundbreaking studies in the field of mathematics, physics, and optics; most of which are still the foundation of their respective fields today.

"I had discovered my element, and, in many respects, the beginning of what I had seen in vision 1700 years earlier. I began collecting every scrap of information I could get my hands on. I moved from country to country within Europe, never tiring of new ideas and new thought. I loved what I was reading and hearing: humans were finally using their brains instead of their bodies. Although not all the information I gathered was accurate, at least it promoted thinking, and reason. Truly, I had reached the age of enlightenment."

"So, do you think that's why you're still alive, to become enlightened?" I asked.

"You pose a good question," he answered thoughtfully. "But no, I think my life was spared solely because I asked for it to be spared. By all accounts, I should have died 1900 years ago. But by the same token, I think that's why everyone is alive, so they can become enlightened."

I studied his face for a minute to try to discern some form of hesitation, or discontinuity in what he had said. His eyes reflected nothing but pure honesty. He was most definitely sincere. It knotted my stomach.

"I'd better get home," I said. "I'll be back tomorrow."

"I'll be waiting," he answered slowly.

24.
COMING TO AMERICA

"Not being known doesn't stop the truth from being true."
- Richard Bach (1936-)

The following evening began just as the last three had, with me questioning his sanity, and him picking up where he'd left off.

"Toward the end of the nineteenth century I found myself migrating south again. I suppose I was on my way back to Madagascar, but I never made it. The Boer War had broken out, and I made my home along the Eastern coast of Africa near a village known today as Maputo.

"One evening, as I sat by my lamp reading, a knock came at my door. I was alarmed to find an exhausted British soldier, tattered and bleeding, standing there, begging for my assistance. As fate would have it, I was the only non-African around, and he had chosen to knock on my door. Whether it was an act of luck, or he had seen me earlier in the day, I don't know. But I do know that he had made the right decision.

"After I had ushered him in and assured him I would do him no harm, I fed him and he rested on my bed. He then revealed to me his story. He told me he had enlisted in London as a press correspondent for the Morning Post, and had been assigned to cover the front of the war, currently in Pretoria. He'd been assigned for less than a month when he was captured by the Boers and made a prisoner of war.

"He told me he had escaped by climbing a ten foot fence that was no less than fifteen feet away from a sentry. He then leapt on an eastbound train and jumped off at first sight of water. He then made his way on foot, east for five more days, traveling by night and resting by day.

"He begged for my assistance to help him reach Delagoa Bay, which I knew well. I accompanied him that very night to the Bay, where he met up with a British regiment, and was eventually reassigned to Natal, to continue reporting the war.

"His parting words to me were unforgettable: 'God bless you, sir. Should we happenstance to meet in the future, I will repay in kind.'

"We embraced and I committed his words to memory; for I knew that in time I would require his assistance, and I knew that he would indeed remember me, and that he would be true to his word.

"Forty years passed. World War II was drawing to a close, and I found it to be a good time to make a permanent move west, to the land of the free and the home of the brave. I made my final pass up the Eastern coast of Africa and westward across Europe to the United Kingdom. I made a brief stay in London until one day my opportunity to cross to America came to fruition.

"A victory parade was scheduled for the Allied Forces' imminent defeat of the Empire of Japan, and I attended. Toward the latter end of the parade, I caught the eye of the hero of the parade and he directed his driver to stop. Although the man was being celebrated that day, I could see he was very heavy-hearted. Apparently, his allies in America and Russia wanted to continue the offensive, whereas he thought it an appropriate time to bring the boys back home.

"He leaned forward and whispered something in one of his guards' ears as he pointed a stubby finger directly at me. The guard made his way to my side and said, 'You have been invited to attend a luncheon at Buckingham Palace immediately following the parade.'

"I attended that luncheon where my favor was indeed repaid in full. Sir Winston Churchill signed and sealed a request to the President of the United States of America, Franklin Delano Roosevelt, to give the man bearing the note anonymous asylum within the borders of the United States. He even went so far as to reserve a spot for me aboard the military ship USS West Point to ensure my safe arrival in the states. My move west had been assured.

"I arrived in Boston on December 3, 1945. The Immigration Department kept me in a holding cell overnight while the authenticity of my request was verified. I don't suppose they got too many requests that were authentic from the likes of Winston Churchill. After it was validated, I was assigned an ambassador who waited on me hand and foot while I completed the required documentation.

"I chose to forego my previous identity as Prester John, and simply go by the initials 'JP' – indicating John Prester. I looked like I was thirty-two, so when the immigration officials asked me my date of birth, I simply stated the truth: June 12, 13. My birth certificate was notarized, and my life as a citizen of the United States began. So, at the age of one thousand nine hundred and thirty-two, I was officially born."

"So what did you do once you arrived in the states?" I asked.

"I'd rather not give too many details on what I've done in the United States, other than the fact that I've taken residence in New York, Florida, Colorado, and now Montana. I keep renewing my Florida plates because it's less paperwork to do, and doesn't leave a paper trail. If word got out that a two thousand year old man was living in Montana, particularly with my history, whether people believed me or not, my life on Patmos would seem comforting. There are very few people who know my true identity, and I prefer to keep it that way."

"How many people know who you really are?" I asked.

"Counting you and I, who are alive, there are two," he grinned.

"Did you tell Sarala?" I asked.

"I would have, eventually, but I never got the chance." He shook his head slowly, reminiscing again. "There's no way it would have worked. I don't know what I was thinking."

"Did you tell Mr. Churchill?" I asked.

"I didn't need to," he responded. "I hadn't aged at all in over forty years since I had last seen him. He was a firm reader and believer in the Bible. I'm certain he knew who I was and he respected the position of maintaining my anonymity."

"Speaking of which," he continued, "I know what you must be thinking right now, and I understand it more than you know, but I would ask you to please tell no one, including Gwen, for a couple more days, until I've had a little bit more time to clarify myself."

It didn't take me very long to decide that I was okay with that idea. I don't know if I'd have told Gwen, anyway. I generally kept my fanatical ideas, of which I had many, to myself, for fear that she'd think I'd lost my mind. This one, however, would top the charts on fanaticism.

"I have no problem with that," I responded. "I'll see you tomorrow then?"

"I'll be waiting," he replied. "Bryce?"

"Yeah?"

"I'm not a freak."

"I don't think you are one, but I do think you may need help; and I'm not sure I'm the one who can give it to you. I'll see you tomorrow." And with that I hobbled down the steps toward my own little slice of reality.

25.
PONDERING HIS STORY

"The highest form of ignorance is when you reject something you don't know anything about."
- Wayne Dyer (1940 -)

Numb. That's the only word I can think of to describe the way I felt. Physically, mentally, and emotionally numb. I slouched at the dinner table over my slab of barbecued chicken. There were conversations going on around me that I did not hear; just low rumblings from around the table. I frequently have the habit of tuning out the world around me so that I can isolate my thoughts. Tonight was one of those nights. During the course of my self-isolation, I surmised three possibilities:

1) JP was lying, and he knew that he was lying.
2) JP was lying, and he didn't know that he was lying.
3) JP was telling the truth.

There is a quality, a sureness, which resonates in someone's voice when they are recalling memories. That quality was in JP's voice tonight. He was not simply regurgitating facts; he was speaking from memory. The more I thought about it, the more I believed that he believed, which is not to say that I believed. I probably would have come to that same conclusion without the assistance of our discussion this evening, because he was my friend, and I trusted him. There was no need to consciously lie, nor did I believe it was in his nature. I therefore discounted possibility number one.

I then addressed possibility number two. How can someone tell such an astounding lie, and not even know they were lying? Is it possible to study something so hard for so long that you eventually come to believe that what you're studying is your own life? These two questions got into some mental issues that I simply did not have the understanding to answer. If this were the case, and I knew it, how could I possibly convince him that he's not who he believes he is? Wouldn't that cause more damage than good - kind of like waking someone when they're sleepwalking? Too many questions.

The third possibility, which I cringed at the thought of even entertaining, brought up even more questions. Is there even a remote possibility that his story is true? Is what he's saying consistent with what I know, and what history shows, to be true? In the extremely unlikely event that his story is true, why on earth would he be telling it to me? And why would he even come here in the first place? What could I offer him that he couldn't find anywhere else? The more I thought about it, the more frustrated I became.

The one thought that kept popping into my head was what was concerning me the most, though. That thought: 'Truth is stranger than fiction'. For some reason, the double meaning of the word 'stranger' kept creeping back into my thoughts.

I was aroused from my stupor by a tiny face brushing against my shoulder.

"Are you finished, Daddy?" My youngest asked, reaching to clear my plate from the table.

I glanced at my plate and realized I had actually been shoving food into my mouth sometime between now, and when I had first sat down at the table.

"Yes, sweetie, you can take my plate," I replied.

There was not going to be a simple solution to this issue. There were too many unanswered questions. Patience is a virtue, I reminded myself, as I excused myself from the table.

26.
TIME WOUNDS ALL HEALS

"If real is what you can feel, smell, taste and see, then 'real' is simply electrical signals interpreted by your brain. "
                                    - Morpheus, from <u>The Matrix</u> (1999)

The next day, I had pre-determined that I was purposely going to avoid the obvious line of questions that were blazing their way through my brain. Instead, I thought it might make things easier for both him and me if I were to lead the conversation, rather than him. I think it caught him off guard, but I also think it relieved him a bit. If there was one thing he had taught me, it was not to dwell too long on one subject without taking a break. We needed a break.

"Do you watch much television?" I asked.

He chuckled and shook his head slowly. "No, I don't. As a matter of fact, I do all that I can to avoid television. The only reason I own one is so I can watch the news."

"I don't blame you," I nodded. "But I saw something a while ago that I've been meaning to ask you about, and with your confiding in me and all, well, I figured maybe I could confide in you a little bit."

"I would be honored," he welcomed.

"When I was about twelve, I watched an episode of <u>The Twilight Zone</u> that made quite an impression on me. It was only about a twenty-minute segment, but I remember it quite vividly, some twenty-five years later.

"It began with a beautiful landscape of yellow and white flowers carpeting a rolling hillside. Nestled amongst the flowers were a man and his wife, with their two little brunette daughters, having a picnic. The sun was shining and everything seemed to be perfect. As the man watched his two daughters play among the flowers, the camera took the angle of what the man was seeing. At first, it was very peaceful and comforting, but as he watched, it was almost as if what he was watching became a television screen, and the picture on the screen was picking up a lot of black static. The man kept shaking his head, to try to clear up what he was seeing, but nothing he did seemed to help at all. The more he tried, the more 'static' appeared in what he was seeing, until eventually he no longer saw his daughters playing on the hillside at all, but a wall of blackness in front of him.

"The camera angle switched again, this time to the blackness, looking at the man as he stood half naked, draped in a towel, in what appeared to be a glass coffin, with several tubes and knobs attached to it. Out of the blackness, two men appeared, both dressed somewhat like mechanics. One of the men said to the other, 'Looks like number 41 is on the fritz again.' He then jiggled some of the wires and tubes leading into the glass coffin, and the camera once again changed viewpoints; this time back into the man's head as he sat in the field of yellow and white flowers with his wife.

"He once again shook his head, to clear the black static, although there wasn't any. The camera paused for a moment as a look of disbelief swept across his face. Then the camera pulled back for one last look at the rolling countryside and the screen faded, ending the show.

"There was nothing about it that was scary, it was just so strange, and very well written and directed. It made me wonder if sometime I'm just going to wake up in a different reality and my life will have been just some dream that I was programmed to have."

"That makes life seem somewhat meaningless, if it is all a dream," he offered.

"So you don't see that as a true representation of reality?" I asked.

"Maybe someone's, but I just don't see how God could judge us for eternity based on a dream," he responded.

"I think our lives are all very real. I picture life as one of those glass globes full of water that you shake up and watch it snow. We live in one, and there's someone on the outside that is very much controlling how much, or how little snow we get in our own little glass globes. When we die, we'll be able to see the globe we lived in; and how we handled the snowstorms.

"It's interesting though, but I keep having a thought pass through my mind that somewhat resembles your story," he added.

"Out with it," I taunted.

"You're going to think this is another feeble attempt at humor, but I actually don't think it's as funny as I do profound; although I think its intent was to be humorous.

He cleared his throat. "When I first moved to Missoula, I was browsing the humor section at Waldenbooks when the cover of a National Lampoon cartoon book caught my eye. It was a very simple cartoon that didn't even have a caption, nor did it need one. The cartoon depicted a medieval torture chamber, with a bearded man who had obviously been there for quite some time, suspended by his wrists from chains, hanging about a foot above the ground against a solid rock wall. About three feet in front of him was another solid rock wall, which he was staring at. Hanging at eye level directly in front of his face was a clock:

"That cartoon depicted my view of life," he said sadly.

"Hey, man, it can't be that bad," I added, in a feeble attempt to cheer him up.

"It's not," he said. "I just haven't been able to shake that cartoon from my head. There's a lot of truth to it."

Silence. I couldn't think of anything to say.

Finally, he continued, "Einstein defined relativity by stating: 'When you are courting a nice girl an hour seems like a second. When you sit on a red-hot cinder a second seems like an hour.' I have my 'courting' days, and I have my 'cinder' days. Everybody does."

"So, since you've met me, would you say you've had more 'courting' or 'cinder' days?" I asked, mostly serious.

"They don't have to be days," he surprised me, "they can be moments. And let me just say that you've provided me with several 'courting' moments."

"Shucks," I mocked, "I'm flattered."

"Well, you should be," he responded seriously. "You're a good man."

"As are you," I sobered up. "And speaking of good men, I think it's time I went home and tried to be a good husband and father. My son has a Cub Scout awards banquet I need to go to. I'd better get going. I'll see you tomorrow."

He voiced through hushed breath, "I'll be waiting."

27.
INQUIRING MINDS

"I have no particular talent. I am merely inquisitive. "
- Albert Einstein (1879 - 1955)

The next day, I was pleased when he gave me the opportunity to ask him the questions that were bouncing around in my head. For the most part, I had remained silent while he had rehearsed to me what he believed to be his life, which, according to him, spanned the greater part of 2000 years. I guess that was mostly because I was trying to think of how I should handle the whole situation, rather than concentrating on what he was saying.

The gist of the problem was that I knew he knew his facts, and I didn't. Asking factual questions would be pointless. If I were to 'expose' him, it would be through feelings, or thoughts, not facts. There was no particular order, or cohesion to my questions. I simply fired away.

"What did you do in your spare time?" I asked.

"When?" Was his rather predictable reply.

"Whenever," I said. "You pick."

He pondered a moment and gave a somewhat all-inclusive answer to my somewhat all-inclusive question.

"There have been three consistencies through the ages," he mused, "people, food, and art. All three have changed drastically over time, but in the sense that they have not died, they are consistent. They always will be. Toward the latter end of the sixteenth century, I would have to add education to that list. Ironically enough, the world of art made its most remarkable change at roughly the same time.

"My first 1600 years or so I spent with people. They took up the bulk of my spare time, as they should. I concentrated on my missionary work, and I enjoyed that. My last 400 I have mainly concentrated on my education, although the missionary work has continued."

"You're still a missionary?" I asked.

"Of course. Jesus' command to us, the apostles, didn't die with his crucifixion. I will always feel a sense of obligation and duty to continue to fulfill His request," he stated.

I gestured with my hands to our surroundings. "How is this considered missionary work?" I asked.

"There are new methods," he grinned. "The old days of standing on milk cartons on street corners have long since died out. I believe you're familiar with the Internet. I've discovered that my laptop computer works quite effectively as a teaching tool; and it helps me maintain my anonymity. And best of all, they come to me, I don't need to go to them."

"You have an Internet site?" I balked.

"Not just one," he clarified, "more like a hundred."

"What are their names?"

He wagged his finger at me. "Nice try."

"At least give me their subject matter," I followed up.

"Topics include almost everything you can name," he said. "My philosophy is that when you hear truth, you will recognize it. I think with your background in computers, and your unquenchable curiosity, you will definitely come across one or more of them sooner or later, if you haven't already."

"I'll bet you have one about God," I beamed.

He smiled. "That's a fairly safe bet." Then he quoted: "Seek, and ye shall find."

I waited a moment and then prodded him to continue with our original discussion.

"You were saying: people, food, and art…"

"Ah, yes," he continued. "Voltaire once said: 'Nothing would be more tiresome than eating and drinking if God had not made them a pleasure as well as a necessity.' What a powerful thought. The consistencies that I'm talking about could very well be a burden to our everyday lives if there wasn't an element of pleasure in them. It's these consistencies that carry us, me, through our daily lives looking forward to tomorrow."

"I have Bell's Palsy," I said. "When it first set in, I lost the use of my taste buds for two days. I was miserable. Eating was a chore."

"My point exactly," he said.

It was silent for a moment as he formulated his thoughts.

"I used the term 'art', but for me, I have focused more on the music aspect of 'art'. It doesn't matter what mood I'm in, there is always a song that can match that mood, if I seek it out. That's an amazing thing when you think about it."

"So what's your favorite song?" I followed up.

"Somehow I knew that was coming," he said. "There's a new favorite with every mood. But to narrow it down, Beethoven, to me, represents the age of enlightenment, and the time in my life I enjoyed the most. The person I cared the most for was Sarala. If I combine these two concepts, I arrive at the Adagio from Beethoven's Piano Sonata No. 8, Opus 13, Pathetique. It's lovely. It always reminds me of Sarala. But, ask me again tomorrow, and I may give you a different answer."

"How come you don't have a stereo?" I wondered.

"Too bulky," he replied. " I pack light. Right now, I'm in more of a reading mode than a listening mode. I can always find something to listen to on my pocket radio, should I feel inclined. That, too, is subject to change, however."

I changed modes. "You've seen the future. Have you ever changed it?"

"Somewhat of an oxymoron, there," he said. "If I could change the future, it wouldn't be the future, would it?

I would have seen something other than the future, a possible future, perhaps. But, I understand your question.

"I've often thought about what 'might have been' if I'd have turned Winston Churchill over to the African authorities. He might never have gone on to be the leader of England. Hitler might have conquered England. The list goes on, and becomes quite scary, really.

"But don't misunderstand my intentions. I look forward to the end. I closed the Book of Revelations by beckoning Jesus to return quickly. Any action I take to deter what will be might prolong the inevitable. What I have seen *will* happen, and I can do nothing to change that. But that is definitely not my intent, nor my purpose. I must watch and wait, just like you."

"Have you ever changed it by mistake?" I followed up.

"Not any more than you have," he answered quietly.

28.
RANDOM QUESTIONS

"I saw the angel in the marble and I chiseled until I set it free."
- Michelangelo (1475 - 1564)

"Tell me about Jesus," I said, as I shifted my weight in the chair.

"Actually, I already have," he responded. "I wrote a book about Him that I'm guessing you've already read, it's called, The Gospel According to St. John."

"That's a cop-out," I sneered. "Tell me something new. Tell me something nobody else knows."

"Before I tell you something new, I want to express to you something you probably already know, but don't know the extent. We live in a time when a man simply cannot tell another man that he loves him, especially in public. I was raised in a time when it was not only spoken, it was shown. Everything about Jesus exuded love. He hugged, He held, He kissed. To somehow mingle that with what today has become synonymous with the word 'gay' is blatantly inaccurate. Jesus embodied love. He would never be ashamed to show it, then, or now."

He thought for a moment. "But to answer your question, perhaps I should begin by telling you that if He were here today, and I should happen to buy Him a gift, I would get Him a pet bulldog."

"A bulldog..." I mumbled.

"Yes. I've had quite a lot of time to think about it, and I have come to the conclusion that He would probably really like to have a pet bulldog - perhaps a white one with black spots."

"And your logic behind that would be..." I mumbled again.

"Basically, I think it would be the perfect gift because in His lifetime He seemed to surround himself with bulldogs; even showing somewhat of a favoritism toward them."

"I take it we're not talking about dogs," I concluded.

He nodded in agreement.

"That is correct. Look at the people who were the closest to Him, the people that He confided the most in: Peter, James, and me. The Bible is full of references to our collective stubbornness. Peter had a bit of an expletive problem, hacked off a man's ear, and denied that he even knew Jesus three times. James and I acquired the nickname 'Boangeres' – meaning 'The Sons of Thunder' - due to our bull-headedness and inexperience. At one point, my brother and I fully intended to call down fire from heaven to consume a village of Samaritans, not exactly what Jesus had in mind. Jesus rebuked us for our behavior, yet still saw in us whatever it was that He entrusted us to head His church upon His death.

"I think that's what I would tell you was Jesus' most misunderstood trait: His ability to not see you, per se, but to see *through* you to what you could become. He then treated you as if you were already that person. That's why I think He'd like a bulldog - He would admire the stubbornness and feistiness that they exude, and He would enjoy the challenge of channeling that aggression toward a single worthy cause."

"Did you all get along? You and the eleven apostles, I mean," I asked.

"No, not at all. As a matter of fact, there were several occasions when we fought like cats and dogs. Were it not for Jesus, we would probably never have had anything to do with each other. His leadership bonded us. It wasn't until after His resurrection that we began to see eye-to-eye, and I think that was due to the collective fear that enveloped us, caused by the loss of our leader."

"Have you read The Da Vinci Code?" I threw him a curve ball.

"I have," he affirmed, with a curl of a smile forming on his lips.

"Then you must know where I'm heading with this," I offered.

"Lay it on me, anyway," he dared.

"Was Jesus married, and to whom?"

He shifted in his chair as if he were a little uncomfortable with my question. It was the first time I'd ever seen this side of him.

"Well, let's take a logical approach to your question," he said. "As I see it, there are three possibilities. Either:

1) Jesus *wasn't* married, thus the Bible is accurate in its omission of mentioning His marriage, as it contains no references to Him being married, or,

2) Jesus *was* married, and it *was* mentioned in the Bible, but for some reason all references to His being married were removed from the text during translation, or at some other time, or,

3) Jesus *was* married, and for some reason none of the authors of the New Testament mentioned it.

"Number one needs no explanation. Number two, as is addressed in The Da Vinci Code, could possibly be because the King James' translators needed to justify the lack of the sacred feminine in the church as it existed in the middle ages. Painstaking efforts would have been taken to camouflage, even alter, the original Greek and Latin texts to eliminate all references to such a marriage, if it did indeed exist.

"Number three requires even more thought, though. It begs the question, 'Why would the New Testament authors purposely avoid mentioning Jesus' marriage?' I think the logical answer to that question is: perhaps they were told specifically *not* to mention it. There are several references in the Bible, such as 2 Corinthians 12: 3-4, where an author says something to the affect that they saw more than they were allowed to write at that time. Perhaps this would be one of those times."

"You didn't answer my question," I stated sharply.

"I *can't* answer your question," he replied, equally as sharp.

Silence. I knew that in not answering my question, he had answered my question. Due to the nature of his third argument, I decided that he respected certain peoples' requests to a larger degree than he respected my right to have my curiosity satisfied. It was a catch-22 that he had handled rather well. Perhaps it wasn't the first time he had addressed such a question.

"So what did you think of The Da Vinci Code?" I switched gears.

"I think it was a fascinating story that inspired people to think. From that standpoint alone, I think it was worth the read. I think the author, Dan Brown, missed an interesting concept as long as he was deriving his own conclusions, however."

"How so?" I asked.

"Do you remember the scripture I showed you, John 21:22, where the disciple whom Jesus loved is granted to tarry until Jesus comes again?"

"Yes, quite well," I replied. (It hadn't left my mind for the last two days.)

"Well, if that disciple was Mary Magdalene, then the quest for the Holy Grail would be all the more important, wouldn't it? With Mary being still alive and all, they wouldn't be seeking the posterity of the Grail, they would be seeking the Grail itself. It would have added a bit of drama to the story – not that it needed it."

"Interesting," I pondered. "But you know that it wasn't Mary that Jesus was speaking to, don't you?"

"Yes I do, and I hope you will come to know it, too."

"I'm working on it," I replied as I stood up from the chair. "I'll catch you tomorrow."

"I'll be waiting."

29.
THE GOOD BOOK

"A bookstore is one of the only pieces of evidence we have that people are still thinking."
                                             - Jerry Seinfeld (1954 -)

"You've referenced the Bible several times," I started, "I'm assuming that means you believe it to be true?"

He bowed his head and looked at the floor of the porch for a moment, unsure how he should reply to my question. After several deep-cleansing breaths, he sat back as a sly grin pursed his lips.

"You ask some difficult questions. The concise, undefined answer to your question is, yes, I believe it to be true. But I need to clarify my answer, and it may take the duration of our time together today."

"You in a hurry?" I joshed.

"No, no, I'm not," he smiled.

He bent down and grasped the Bible, which these days was a common prop for our discussions, and he frequently had it by his side before I ever came over. He held it up and asked me what I saw.

"The Holy Bible, King James Version," I replied, reading the cover.

"And how many copies would you say you have in your house?" He asked.

"Probably three or four," I remarked, wondering where he was heading with this.

"And what can you tell me about King James?" He prodded again.

"Um, he was probably a king," I chuckled.

"Anything else...?"

"...Of England?" I guessed.

He waited a moment for emphasis, and to let me think, as he always did after he had asked a question and was about to make a point.

"Don't you think it's odd that you have three or four copies of a book in your home, and you can't tell me the first thing about how it came to be?"

"I've never really thought about it, but yes, that is quite odd," I replied.

"Well you're not alone," he said. "I'd venture a guess to say that less than one percent of the people who own the King James Version of <u>The Holy Bible</u> can tell me any more than you just did: possibly way less than one percent. It's been the best selling book for almost 400 years, currently selling over 100 million copies a year, and precious few people know the story of its origin."

"So help me become part of the less than one percent," I said excitedly.

He took a deep breath and scratched at his stomach. "It'd be nice to begin by saying that King James was a most noble and righteous man, but that would start our story with a lie. The truth of the matter is that he was a callous, immoral, power-hungry man.

"He was born the son of Mary, Queen of Scots, who was at the time the Queen of Scotland, but sought to become the rightful heir to the throne of England; to which she succeeded. Upon her abdication of the throne of Scotland, James took her place. He became 'King James VI of Scotland'.

"There are many who said of James that he showed little or no remorse when his mother was beheaded; probably because it brought him that much closer to the throne of England. Indeed, after the death of Queen Elizabeth I of England, Mary's successor, James did have right to the throne of England. He dropped the title 'King James VI of Scotland', and assumed the title 'King James I of England', in the year 1603.

"He was immediately confronted with the problem of the division of the Church of England into two different sects, the Conformists, who were satisfied with things as they were, and the Puritans, who wanted things to get better. In an attempt to restore some semblance of peace to the nation, James held a conference at Hampton Court Palace in January of 1604 to try to unify the two divisions. For the most part, the conference was a bust; but a single common ground was discovered between the two parties: the need for a new version of an English Bible. Dr. John Reynolds, who was at the time the President of Corpus Christi College, recommended to the King that one be created.

"King James organized a party of fifty-four scholars and educated men to establish a new version of the Bible. He gave them fifteen 'rules' to follow while compiling the new translation. In general, the rules stated that they were to break into six groups, each taking a different section of the Bible's that existed at the time (Tyndale's, Coverdale's, Matthew's, Whitchurch's, Geneva, and the Greek Textus Receptus), along with scrolls, notes, and any other information they could get their hands on, and translate each section. When they had completed that section, they would pass it on to the next group, and they would translate that same section, until all of the groups had translated all of the sections. Then they would convene, and compare the various translations and agree on one final translation, until the whole of the Bible had been completed.

"For some unexplained reason, the translating did not actually get under way until 1607. Only forty-seven of the fifty-four men that were asked actually participated in the translation process, but the forty-seven were men of great renown, and highly esteemed as most reputable. It's interesting to note that King James did not actually finance the project, because he plead poverty at the time. In reality, the project was funded by the most well to do bishops of the day.

"The project lasted two years and nine months. Upon completion, the entire manuscript was presented back to the King for his approval. King James wasn't quite sure what to do with it, so he passed it on to Sir Francis Bacon, his Chief Advisor to the Crown, for evaluation.

"Allow me to add my own personal opinion at this point in our tale that this was an ingenious move on the King's part. Sir Francis Bacon was one of the most brilliant men ever to walk the face of the Earth. Among other things, Sir Bacon is known today as the Father of several branches of science; principally due to the fact that he invented a process known as 'inductive reasoning' – which is the basis of exploration of almost all branches of modern science. It involves a series of logical questioning, much like your own, that leads to more questions, until the topic in doubt has been validated, or disproved.

"There are also some who think that Sir Bacon is the true author of the Shakespearean works. From everything I've ever read, I see no reason to disagree with that speculation, although there is no concrete evidence to the affirmative.

"Anyway, Sir Francis Bacon had the original translation in his possession for over a year. During that time, he wrote prefaces and synthesized the language of the original translation into the fluid Old English language that we, the reader's of the Bible, have become so familiar with today. There are some who say that he also encoded secret information into the text, which can never be verified, because the original translated version has not been seen since 1665.

"Sir Bacon then returned his final manuscript to King James, with his approval. The King ordered a dedicatory page to be drawn up in his honor. In addition, he decreed that this new version of the Bible was to be "read in the churches" – thus unifying the beliefs of the two divisions within the Church of England.

"More than 100,000 changes have occurred to the original text released to the public in 1611, most of which are language changes, like changing thousands of 'i's' to 'j's'; such as in the word 'maiesty', changing to the word 'majesty'. There were, however, a few blatant printing errors, such as the misspelling of the word 'he' as 'she'. There was also a case where the word 'Jesus' was accidentally replaced with the word 'Judas'. That was the most obvious error that occurred in the original translation.

"There are those who believe that since the King James Version contains the words 'Authorized' and 'Original', that it means the Book contains the original translation of the Greek to English; but this is not the case, at all. The original Greek was not even translated until the fourth century, and even then it was translated from Hebrew and Aramaic. So what we have as the 'Authorized' and 'Original' version is really translations from the original Hebrew and Aramaic to Greek to Latin to English, and finally to Old English. And, of course, we do an additional translation in our heads every time we read it, because we don't speak Old English.

"There is also a built-in misunderstanding in the order of the Books in the New Testament. To the unknowing, the Books appear to be in chronological order; but that too, is inaccurate. Right now, the New Testament appears in this order, which was originally assembled by a man named Jerome around 400 A.D."

He took the pen from his shirt pocket and scrawled the following on a piece of scrap paper:

1) Matthew
2) Mark
3) Luke
4) John
5) Acts
6) The General Epistles
7) The Pauline Epistles

8) The Revelation of St. John

"No-one knows for sure what Jerome was thinking when he compiled the manuscripts. They are, very roughly, in chronological order, although to be precise, if they were ordered chronologically, they would fall in the following order:

1) Mark (55 A.D.)
2) Matthew (58 A.D.)
3) Luke (61 A.D.)
4) Acts (63 A.D.)
5) The General Epistles (50 A.D. – 68 A.D.)
6) The Pauline Epistles (50 A.D. – 68 A.D.)
7) John (70 A.D.)
8) The Revelation of St. John (90 A.D.)

"You might ask 'so what?' - and in most cases knowing this order wouldn't make any difference, but the Bible is also a history book, and history is often a great deal easier to understand when studied chronologically, or at least knowing what preceded what, in terms of events that happened."
"Give me an example," I said.
"Very well. Let's compare three seemingly identical verses written by three different authors of the Gospels," He showed me the following verses in order:

Mark 14:47 – And one of them that stood by drew a sword, and smote a servant of the high priest, and cut off his ear.

Luke 22:50 – And one of them smote the servant of

the high priest, and cut
off his right ear.

John 18:10 – Then Simon
Peter having a sword
drew it, and smote the
high priest's servant, and
cut off his right ear. The
servant's name was
Malchus.

"All three refer to the same event. What are the major differences between the verses?" he asked me.

"John names the man who cut off the servant's ear," I answered quickly.

He gave me a quick glance as if it hurt him that I did not accept the fact that he was indeed the 'John' of which I spoke. "And why would I do that?" he asked.

"I don't know," I answered.

The inevitable silence, then, the answer: "Because Peter was still alive at the time the first two verses were written, and Mark and Luke did not want to incriminate him. For those two men to write down the fact that Peter drew his sword and smote another man, especially a man that held governmental authority, would just add fuel to the fire of what was already a very bitter hatred of Christians by the Romans.

"I, on the other hand, wrote my account twenty years later, after Peter had already suffered a martyr's fate. In essence, I laid the mystery to rest because Peter's death was commonly known, and I may have spared someone false accusation by naming the guilty party. There was no need to be secretive anymore. This is an incredibly simple comparison, but I think you can understand my point. It just helps to know the background while you try to understand the account."

"So why did you write the Book of John in the third person?" I asked.

He was alarmed. Once again I think I stunned him because I knew more than he thought I did.

"Good timing," he replied. "It fits in with my point exactly. If I were to write the Book of John in the first person, I would have, in essence, been incriminating myself. I was, at the time, the only original apostle still alive, and the manhunt was on. There also existed the fact that Jesus did indeed promise at least one of his apostles that he would tarry. At the time, I did not want that to become common knowledge among the people."

"But later, when you wrote Revelations, you used the first person," I protested.

"Exactly my point again," he replied. "I wrote Revelation while I was on the Isle of Patmos, and everyone knew who I was by then, thanks to a reputation of having survived a cauldron of boiling oil. As a matter of fact, I used the first person to assure the saints that I was indeed alive and well, wanting to give them hope.

"So, now that you know the history, I can honestly and more precisely answer your original question, which was: 'Do you believe the Bible to be true?' My answer is an unequivocal 'yes'; provided you read it with the understanding that sufficient thought must be incorporated into the process for your mind to sort out the truth of each passage. I was instructed that the Holy Ghost would teach me the truth of all things. I do not have exclusive rights to this. You have the same right. I would recommend using it. There's a reason why Mary Budd Rowe's research on 'silence as an effective teacher' was so profound. She wasn't the first to employ the principle. Although she may not realize it, Jesus affirmed the principle 1950 years previous, and I believe he obtained his information from a pretty powerful source.

"I want to be clear though, that not *all* truth can be found in the Bible," he continued. "To assume such would be to assume that *all* of the apostle's writings, and *all* of Jesus' teachings are found in the Bible, and they aren't. The Dead Sea scrolls are a classic example: some of them are accurate, some are counterfeits. And, as I pointed out earlier, there were things the apostles were specifically asked not to write about. Is it logical to assume that since I didn't write about it, it must not be true? That's not sound logic. Look at this:"

He flipped through the Bible and pointed to another verse, which he himself had written:

> John 21:25 – And there
> are also many other
> things which Jesus did,
> the which, if they should
> be written every one, I
> suppose that even the
> world itself could not
> contain the books that
> should be written. Amen.

"It is likewise logical to assume that truth can be found within other writings: the Koran, the Talmud, the Torah, or even a can of spray paint. That doesn't necessarily mean they contain all truth; just that truth can be found within them.

"Albert Schweitzer once said: 'Truth has no special time of its own. Its hour is now, always.' That's a profound statement, and ultimately, we must each decide on our own definition of what 'truth' is, and where it comes from. It is likewise crucial that you do not limit yourself to one single source of truth. To do so would be robbing yourself."

I looked at the Bible that he was still clutching in his hand. To a large degree, I felt embarrassed, having known nothing of what he had just told me; but at the same time, there was an air of truth in what he had said that was comforting. I wished I could have been more of a contributor to our conversation, although he didn't seem to mind.

I excused myself and thanked him for his time. He replied that there was plenty more where that came from. It wasn't until I got home that it dawned on me that he wasn't referring to his sermon; he was referring to his time.

30.
CRACKING CODES

"Don't you believe that there is in man a deep so profound as to be hidden even to him in whom it is?"
- St. Augustine (354 -430)

"You mentioned yesterday that Sir Francis Bacon might have worked his own set of codes into the text of the Bible. Do you think he did?"

"Yes," he replied curtly.

"Doesn't that disturb you?" I asked.

"Why would it disturb me?" he asked. "The whole of the Bible is a code, of sorts. I think if Bacon did in fact add anything to the text, it would be nearly impossible to detect, and blend in so naturally that it would not at all detract from the original text."

"What sort of codes are we talking about here?" I wondered.

He let out a sort of smug laugh. "How's your imagination?"

"Try me," I tempted.

He picked up his Bible again as a very sinister gleam sparkled in his eyes. This was his forte.

"The standard terminal notation used in the 46th Psalm is the word 'Selah'. If you omit the word 'Selah' from the entire context of the 46th Psalm, and start from verse one, counting 46 words into the Psalm, you arrive at the word 'shake'. Counting 46 words backward from the end of the Psalm, you arrive at the word 'spear'."

"Here," he said, "see for yourself."

I snatched the Bible from his hands and rummaged through the well-worn pages until I reached the 46th Psalm. One by one I counted the words into the chapter, until I arrived at the 46th word: 'shake'. Then I proceeded to count backwards from the end of the text, skipping the word 'Selah', and I arrived at the word 'spear'.

I gawked. "So what is this supposed to mean?"

"It might not mean anything. It may just be a coincidence. You'll find it interesting to note, however, that our good friend William Shakespeare turned 46 in the year 1610 – the year Sir Francis Bacon did his own little bit of editing to the Old Testament."

Again I repeated, "So what the dump does it mean?"

"Some say that it means Bacon *was* Shakespeare," he said. "But I think that's carrying it a bit too far, don't you? I *do* think it means something, however. It's far too much of a coincidence to just write it off. I'm more prone to believe it was Sir Francis Bacon's way of wishing Shakespeare a happy birthday. At the very least, it's an interesting little anecdote to ponder."

"Did he add any other codes?" I asked.

"Most definitely," he responded. "I'm just not aware of them. I'm sure someday somebody will find them."

"But you said the whole Bible was a code..." I said.

"And it is," he replied. "There are some devout Jews who believe the entire Old Testament is nothing more than an allegory; a figurative explanation for the creation of the world. Almost everything Jesus said was a code; that's what a parable is. The word 'parable' itself comes from the Greek word meaning 'comparison'. Only those who were 'in tune' with Jesus would really know what He was truly saying. To everyone else, parables were merely stories. Jesus himself explained it best when He said, 'Seeing they see not.'

"You could always tell the disciples who truly understood what He taught: they were the ones whose faces were set in deep thought, or the ones with light bulbs going off over their heads. The rest were there merely to hear entertaining stories. And that is truly the beauty of speaking in parables: there's something for everyone."

"And you wrote in codes, too?" I asked.

"I tried to make my letters as clear as possible," he answered.

"I don't understand Revelation," I said. "There's no code there?"

"Yes," he admitted, "Revelation is a code. But that was a necessary code."

"Meaning what?"

"Meaning if I'd have bluntly written everything I saw, the world would be a very different place today," he said.

"How's that?" I asked.

"Do you remember our discussion on death, and if you would want to know how and when you were going to die?" he asked.

"Sure."

"Well, it's along those lines. If I were to blatantly come out and say that the United States would be utterly wasted by nuclear missiles in the year 2014, and that were to find it's way into the Bible, can you imagine the hysteria it would cause? Not to mention the people who would try to 'fulfill prophecy' by creating their own disasters."

"You were correct," he concluded. "Revelation is a code, too. And those who can see, see."

"It's too depressing for me," I admitted.

"Not for me," he said, with a look of deep sadness on his face.

It was somber for a moment, and then he perked up substantially. "If you like puzzles, I've got one for you. Here is a revelation, of sorts, that I had in 1968. At first, I didn't know what to make of it, but as time passed, it became quite clear."

He took his time as he scrawled quite a few words on a scrap of paper. He handed it to me and said, "This'll be your homework for tomorrow."

I glanced at it for a second and noted that it looked very confusing.

"See if you can figure out what it means," he said. "It took me a couple of years, but I'm guessing you can get it tonight."

"I'll try," I said, while I rose to my feet. "But I'm not guaranteeing anything. See you tomorrow."

"I'll be waiting," he said, in typical fashion.

I studied the note as soon as I got home. It was written in the familiar Old English of the Bible:

...And I beheld a banner,
which wielded much power.
The Western-most side of the
banner was tattered and frayed.
The banner thereof was divided
into four quadrants: one
quadrant was bathed in blood,
one in emerald, one of pure
gold, and the last shown as the
ocean. And the banner flew
high for all nations to behold.

What was this? And I was supposed to recognize it? Before tomorrow? I don't think so. So it's a flag. Divided in four. Every nation's flag I could think of was divided into three sections or less. Switzerland, maybe? I was pretty sure their flag was only baby blue and white. And what did JP's seeing it in 1968 have to do with anything? Wasn't that around the year JFK got shot? Maybe that explains the 'bathed in blood' part. I'm no good at this.

I showed it to Gwen and she said it reminded her of war. She suggested that maybe the four quadrants represented four different countries. Maybe the Western-most two countries were losing the war, or at least a lot of people. When I mentioned 1968 to her, she suggested that maybe it was the Viet Nam War.

"Try the Internet," she suggested. "It's not going to hurt anything."

I went down to my study and logged on to the Internet. I plugged in 'Banner' and '1968' as the keywords on my Excite page search engine. Seventy-two hits. This might take all night.

Just then my son Nathan came in and sat down at the kids' computer, which sits opposite mine in the corner of the room. We had had a power outage the night before, so we'd turned off the power. He reached around the monitor and flipped the switch on.

As I sat transfixed over the puzzle looming in front of me, I caught, out of the corner of my eye, the luminescent glow of the computer monitor as it blazed the ever-present Microsoft Windows boot-up screen. I glared in amazement as the four-sectioned flag hung suspended against a clear blue sky; the tattered edges of the flag waning off to the left, or Western-most, portion of the screen.

Perhaps this puzzle wasn't going to take all night.

It was then, at that 'A-ha' moment, that I realized what my friend JP's revelation was. If he had had this clear of a revelation in 1968, what did it mean to him when Microsoft got started, sometime around 1975?

It was then that the true 'A-ha' moment occurred. If, in 1975, JP knew that Microsoft would make it big, he would have no problem at all securing a tidy sum for his investment portfolio. If, in 1968, JP knew that Microsoft would make it big, maybe he *could* see the future.

And maybe JP's name wasn't JP after all.

31.
INTERROGATING MYSELF

"You cannot depend on your eyes
when your imagination is out of focus."
- Mark Twain (1835 - 1910)

Nine days ago, my neighbor affirmed what I judged to be a severe mental illness by proclaiming that he was, in fact, John the Beloved. Due to the nature of our conversations, and indeed, my very friendship with him, I made the decision to disregard the claim and simply tolerate the eccentricity. He was, after all, the most intelligent man I had ever met, and he seemed to enjoy imparting of his wisdom to me. It was certainly not my wish to offend him.

Tonight, I began asking myself the question: 'Why isn't he John the Beloved?" Three immediate answers sprung to my mind:

1) Because people can't live 2000 years.
2) Because if John the Beloved were still alive today, he would be someone else, somewhere else, not living as a common man amongst fellow nobody's.
3) Because John the Beloved, if he were alive, would not choose to live in Missoula, Montana,

as Bryce Anderson's
neighbor.

I began dissecting the items one at a time, starting
with the first item on the list. Weren't there people in the
Old Testament who lived 900 years? I considered myself to
be a Christian. Did I really believe the Old Testament? If
they lived to be 900 then, why not 2000 today?

Did I really believe Jesus was who he said he was, or
was I just professing to be a Christian because that's what
everybody else I knew was doing? What did Jesus mean
when he told one of his apostle's they would tarry until he
came again? Did I believe that? If Jesus could raise himself
from the dead, why couldn't he give someone power over
death so they wouldn't die? Did I believe that? Did I believe
he gave that power to John? Was that person now living
across the street from me?

What *would* John the Beloved be doing today, if he
were still alive? Wouldn't he be the Pope, or Billy Graham,
or some huge religious icon somewhere? Wouldn't he have
a worldwide following and be crying repentance to everyone
he met? Wouldn't everybody know who he was? Wouldn't
being around John the Beloved be akin to being around
Jesus himself? What would it be like to be around Jesus?

Suddenly my mind cleared of the onslaught of
questions and a single word came to my mind: *magnetic*. JP
had used that word to describe Jesus' personality. When I
thought about it, I would use that same word to describe JP.
Magnetic: the sheer exhilaration of being around someone
simply because you enjoy being around them. That
described JP.

What else did I know? I knew he hadn't lied to me
about his name [JP]. I knew the true story behind his birth
certificate, which he had later confirmed. I knew he wasn't
afraid to hug me, or even cry. I knew he was brilliant, and in
no way seemed mentally off base. I knew he had a deep-

seated need for me to believe him, whether he was lying or not.

I knew I liked and trusted him, and I knew he wasn't lying; not on purpose, anyway. Either he was John the Beloved, or he had a severe mental problem. This was the brightest man I'd ever met. I did not believe he had a mental problem. That left only one alternative.

32.
GRAY MATTERS

"If the human mind was simple enough to understand,
we'd be too simple to understand it."
-    Emerson Pugh (1929 -)

The next time we met, I was eager to find out more about his 'revelation'. I opened our conversation with: "So, do you have a portfolio, or just the one stock?"

A sly grin swept across his face as he realized that I had solved his puzzle. He seemed pleased that I'd done it so swiftly.

"My intent is not greed," he responded. "I have enough to live as comfortably as I want to."

"Tell me more about this 'revelation' you received," I prodded.

"Not much to tell, really," he answered. "I woke up one morning and had that picture etched in my mind. I did some research to find out what it was, but of course I found nothing, because it didn't even exist yet. I made a sketch of it, for future reference, but eventually, I let it slip from my conscious mind and went on to other things. It wasn't until eight years later, as I happened by a television set in the marquee of a mall, that I saw a stock report on the news that brought back the long-forgotten memory. I acted quickly, and invested what little money I had, and just kept on re-investing the dividends. It didn't take too long for me to have enough for my purposes."

"How much did you invest?" I asked.

"Enough. Again, my intent was not greed."

I thought for a moment and finally broke the silence with a question I assumed he'd anticipated me asking for quite some time. "You know this is impossible, don't you?"

"What's impossible?" he returned.

"My being able to prove who you are, or aren't," I answered. "It's somewhat of a Catch-22," I added. "I could ask you all the questions I want, and you could answer every one. If I like your answers, I move on to the next question. If I don't like your answers, or they disagree with something I already know or believe, you could simply tell me that what I know or believe is incorrect. Your being my intellectual superior doesn't help my case any, either."

"Do you have something specific in mind?" he asked.

"Well, this stock thing for one," I said. "You could show me your certificates, your bank account, or whatever, to prove you do have Microsoft stock, but that really doesn't prove anything. Maybe you just got lucky and overheard some broker over lunch one day, I don't know. It seems like the only thing that would definitely prove to me that you are who you say you are is the passage of time. In fifty years, if I'm hobbling around with a walker and you still look like you're ready for a racquetball tournament, that would be fairly conclusive, I think. Other than that, there's really no way I can prove, or disprove, who you really are."

"Maybe you're trying too hard," he said. "Give it a rest. Something will come to you. Let me take your mind off of it by telling you about something I've been researching, that I find fascinating."

It seems like it had been forever since I actually learned anything from JP, but it was only yesterday. My mind gets like that sometimes. I dwell so long on a problem that it consumes my life. It affects my mood, my time, my relationships; kind of a 'no rest for the wicked' type thing. I was due for a re-awakening, and this one sounded like a good one: something that JP found fascinating. I kicked my feet up on the porch railing and let him do the talking.

"In 1848, a man named Phineas Gage was working as a construction supervisor for the Rutland and Burland Railroad outside of Cavendish, Vermont. On September 13th of that year, Phineas was preparing a powder charge to blast a rock, and inadvertently used a tamping rod in a hole that had already been set with powder. The resulting explosion blew the tamping rod upwards at an angle through his left cheekbone, through his left eye socket, and out the top, front portion of his head. Ultimately, the rod landed about 25 to 30 yards behind him. The tamping rod was three feet seven inches long, roughly one fourth of an inch wide at one end, and about one inch wide at the other; somewhat like a three-and-a-half foot long metal pool cue.

"Witnesses say that Gage was knocked down, but didn't even lose consciousness; even though the majority of the front left portion of his brain was gone. Gage was taken into Cavendish, where a physician named John Harlow treated him so successfully that Gage returned to his home in New Hampshire about two and a half months later. About six months after that, Gage had recovered enough to want to return to work; but was refused employment on the grounds that he was 'not the same man' that had worked for the company previously.

"It appears that Mr. Gage suffered a fairly severe personality change, due to the placement of where the metal tamping rod had made its way through his brain. Those who knew Gage said he had drastically changed from being personable, efficient, and very capable, to obstinate, profane, and impatient.

"Gage found employment as a stagecoach driver for most of the remainder of his life; which lasted another twelve years. He died in 1861. His body was exhumed in 1867, and his skull, along with the three foot, seven inch metal tamping rod, is housed in the Warren Medical Museum at Harvard University today.

"This was a landmark case for neurologists, because it was the first time the frontal lobes of the brain were associated with personality and social interaction. Some say that this incident may have been the basis of the now obsolete practice of frontal lobotomy, but no evidence has ever been found to support that claim."

He paused for a moment and let the story sink in. This guy sure knew how to get me thinking.

"You're telling me this guy had a three foot long, one inch diameter rod blown through his head, and lived to tell about it?" I shook my head in disbelief.

"Thirteen years," he said. "But what I find so interesting is not so much that he lived, which in and of itself is remarkable, but the fact that he lost a good portion of his brain, and it didn't affect him more than it did. It made me wonder how much of our brains we could lose, and still be 'ourselves'. In essence, how much of our brains do we actually need, and, what's the purpose of the portion of our brains that we 'don't need'?"

"I'm guessing you found an answer," I joked, knowing full well he had.

"Actually, I didn't," he clarified. "Not a concrete one, anyway. You've probably heard the saying that we only use ten percent of our brains. From everything I've seen, this saying probably originated from a misquote of either Albert Einstein or Margaret Mead. The original saying was more to the effect that we 'use only a small percentage of our brains'. I don't know where the figure [ten percent] got attached to the quote, but it was most probably by advertisers wanting to promote their 'brain enhancing' products.

"Most scientists today seem to think we use one hundred percent of our brain; but that doesn't fit very well, either. If that were the case, how could we ever learn anything new? Every time we learned something new, something we used to know would have to 'leave' so something new could take its place. There would never be any room for growth.

"On the other hand, evolution has pretty much taught us that there's no reason why a human, or any animal for that matter, would carry around 90% of a brain that they never use. No, I'm fairly convinced that neither extreme, 10 or 100 percent, is correct."

He backtracked a little bit. "The brain is an amazing thing. It's made up of millions of neurons, which process information. As neurons 'fire', they can actually be photographed now; much like sparks in the dark, allowing scientists to determine which portion of the brain is associated with a particular activity. This allows scientists to, in essence, make maps of our brain. The interesting thing is that no two people have identical 'maps'. For example, a blind person fires many more neurons in the region of their brain that is associated with the sense of smell than a person that has 20/20 vision. This is due to the simple fact that the blind person relies more heavily on the sense of smell than the person with perfect vision. There are documented cases where the brain has actually 'covered' for itself when one portion of the brain isn't functioning properly."

"What do you mean?" I asked.

"Well, I read of an experiment where a woman voluntarily allowed herself to be blindfolded for 100 hours. At the beginning of the experiment, she took a fairly simple Braille test, to see how well her motor functions could decipher patterns of dots embossed on paper. During her initial test, she had her brain 'mapped', and the only portion of the brain 'firing' was the area associated with motor skills, because her fingers were doing all the work. At the end of the experiment, one hundred hours later, while still blindfolded, she retook the test, and was mapped again. This time, in addition to the area of the brain that controlled motor skills firing, the region of the brain that controlled vision was firing equally as often. It was as if, since the eyes had not functioned for 100 hours, the neurons in the portion of the brain responsible for vision had become bored, and were now assisting the motor skills region of the brain. Ironically enough, it was quite conclusive evidence that the brain has a mind of it's own."

"That's amazing," I stammered.

"Science is amazing," he countered. "Have you heard about the new experimental technology called 'Brain Fingerprinting?'"

"No."

"It's quite intriguing, really. The theory is that there are regions of your brain that fire neurons of recognition, known as P300 waves. For example: if I were to show you three separate photographs of women, and one happened to be your wife, the neurons in your brain would fire differently when shown the picture of your wife than they would when shown photographs of the two women you didn't know. That region of your brain could then be mapped, using an electroencephalogram, and used as somewhat of a lie detector, to measure P300 waves, without you having to say a word.

"It's currently being utilized in investigating crimes. A suspect might be told that the victim was murdered, but not told what the murder weapon was. The suspect is then fitted with a headband that detects P300 waves, and shown several pictures of various weapons, one of which is the actual weapon that was used in the murder case. If the suspect emits P300 waves when shown the true murder weapon, it's a fairly clear sign that he has seen the weapon before.

"Problems arise, however, when the case is a highly publicized one. There's nothing saying the suspect hadn't seen the murder weapon on the five-o-clock news. But there are always details of every crime that investigators don't release to the public. Items as insignificant as what type of shirt the victim was wearing can be used as incriminating evidence against the suspect, as long as it can be shown that the suspect recognized the items.

"The nice thing about the test is that it's impossible to 'cheat' on. The results are accumulated without the suspect ever having to say a word. It's all done by recognition the instant the object is presented to the suspect.

Try instantaneously camouflaging your first impression sometime," he chuckled.

"That's pretty cool," I said. "Where'd you hear about it?"

"I read a lot," he answered.

"Sorry, stupid question," I blushed. "It must be getting late. See you tomorrow."

"I'll be waiting."

33.
IF IT MAKES YOU HAPPY

> "Well," said Pooh, "what I like best," and then
> he had to stop and think. Because although
> eating honey was a very good thing to do, there
> was a moment just before you began to eat it
> which was better than when you were, but he
> didn't know what it was called.
>   - A.A. Milne (1882 – 1956)

He's not here today. I guess I just got so accustomed to his being here whenever I come over that I forget that his life doesn't necessarily revolve around me.

The chairs were here, so I parked myself. It's a nice day; typical for Montana Springtime. There are a few light clouds in the sky, and a subtle breeze blowing out of Lolo canyon. The mild fragrance of grass wafts in the air, emanating from about four of my neighbors who are mowing their lawns, which, of course, reminds me that I have once again been neglectful of mine.

And here I sit with my back hunched over, elbows on my knees, looking across the street at my house. For some reason I am reminded of the day Vanessa was born, and I remember sitting by my wife's side as she slept, having just endured about eight hours of labor.

There was a window in front of me, and, for what seems like a moment when there was no time, I sat transfixed as I gazed across the rooftops toward the hills in the distance. I've never been to Pittsburgh, but for some reason I think it would look a lot like what I was seeing. In that moment, I believe God was telling me that my life would never be the same. It wasn't that it was going to be bad, or good, it was just going to be *different*. I would no longer be concerned with my own life as much as those who depended on me.

I twisted a familiar saying I had heard from <u>Sleeping Beauty</u> to match the moment:

Am I happy to be content, or,
am I content to be happy?

Very few people I know are truly happy. I would venture a guess that, if they're happy at all, they're happy to be content. I would certainly classify myself as being content. But happy – I don't think so; that carries too much of a permanency that, maybe in error, I have attached to 'true happiness'. The strange thing is that being content and being happy are two completely different things: but maybe not in this case.

Several years ago, Gwen and I went on a Caribbean cruise with the Dalfonso's and Gunnell's. We took a day's excursion from the ship to climb the step-like waterfalls of Ocho Rios, Jamaica. The climb was fun, but after the climb, we, the men of the group, took some time out to 'play' in the falls.

One waterfall in particular was about six and a half feet high, and we took the liberty of bracing ourselves against it as we tried to shoulder the burden of the water thrusting down on our upper backs. Again, there was a sense that I was simply not aware of the concept of 'time'. I didn't care what was going on anywhere else in the world: I was happy. Gwen snapped a picture of 'that perfect moment'. Buried somewhere behind all that water, was the largest smile I've conjured in quite a while. To this day, I keep that photograph on my desk next to a picture of my children. During the course of monotonous business days, it provides an instantaneous vacation.

Oscar Levant said: "Happiness isn't something you experience, it's something you remember." Sometimes I think I'm too wrapped up in trying to experience happiness that I try too hard. Looking back it's easy; looking in the present is nearly impossible, for me at least.

The thing is, I'm happier now than I've been in a long time, now that I've discovered my new friend. I guess it just took his absence for me to be aware of that.

I hope he's here tomorrow.

34.
BACK TO THE FUTURE

"There comes a time when the mind takes a higher plane of knowledge but can never prove how it got there."
- Albert Einstein (1879 - 1955)

"I wanted to tell you something the other day, but never quite got around to it," he said. "Do you mind if I show you another scripture?"

"Why would I mind?" I asked.

His answer caught me off guard, especially coming from someone who claimed to have spent the majority of his life preaching.

"It's just that some people get offended if you dwell on the Bible too much. It's not my intention to push anything on you, but rather, to just share some of my thoughts. You're free to take them or leave them as you wish."

"You base a lot of your thoughts on the Bible, don't you?" I pondered.

"A lot of the Bible is based on my thoughts," he replied.

I gave him a quizzical look and grinned a bit. Regardless of who this guy is, or thinks he is, I liked him.

"My style was never to bludgeon anyone with information. I just like to provide it."

"You do it well," I said.

"I had a good teacher," he responded as he flipped open his Bible and held it open for me to see.

"The Book of Ecclesiastes was written by Solomon, the son of King David. The whole book is only 222 verses, and the word 'I' is used 87 times in 65 of those verses; so it's quite easy to see that the book was written as somewhat of an autobiography of how Solomon obtained his wisdom.

It's also important to note that in this verse, the phrase 'under the sun' is synonymous with the term 'in this world'. Check this out:

> Ecclesiastes 1:9 The thing
> that hath been, it is that
> which shall be; and that
> which is done is that
> which shall be done: and
> there is no new thing
> under the sun.

"Pretty complicated, huh?" he asked.

"I don't understand the tense changes," I said.

"You're not alone. Here, " he said, "maybe this will clear it up a little."

He turned a page.

> Ecclesiastes 3:15 That
> which hath been is now;
> and that which is to be
> hath already been; and
> God requireth that which
> is past.

I thought about it for a minute, and then asked the only question that seemed like it might clarify what I thought he was driving at. "Is this referring to reincarnation?"

"No, quite the contrary," he said. "As a matter of fact, I'm still continuing the conversation we had yesterday. One more verse, bear with me."

He flipped back to the previous page and placed his finger under the following verse:

> Ecclesiastes 1:11 There is
> no remembrance of

former things; neither
shall there be any
remembrance of things
that are to come with
those that shall come
after.

It was silent. I read the verse two more times. The first half of the verse made sense. The second half went back to switching tenses again. I was confused: how can we have a remembrance of things that are to come?

He sensed my frustration. I knew it was breaking precedent for him to bludgeon me with a direct answer, but that's what I wanted him to do. I wasn't going to see through this one without some prodding of some sort. Eventually, it came.

"Here," he said, handing me the dictionary. "Let's look up the word 'memory'."

memory: noun. The mental
faculty of storing past
experiences and recalling
them at will.

"So what would it mean that we have 'no remembrance of things that are to come'?" he asked me.

"Using this definition, it would mean that we can't recall the future," I said, realizing I had just changed tenses in the middle of my sentence.

"Which would indicate what?" he asked.

"That the future is hidden somewhere in our brain, we just can't...access it..." I stammered.

He grinned. "Fascinating concept, isn't it?"

"So what does it take to access it?" I asked.

"It's probably different for everyone, but I would assume some of the essential ingredients are desire, study, silence, and meditation. My theory is that the 'A-ha' moment, of which you and I have spoken on several occasions, is nothing more than a sigh of relief given off by neurons in your brain that have long awaited you to uncover them, and you finally have."

He added, "It also very realistically explains the phenomenon of the term 'déjà vu'. I've always thought the relationship between the 'A-ha moment' and déjà vu was very close."

"If what you're saying is correct, our whole lives would be one long 'déjà vu'," I noted.

"And it would make seeing the future somewhat more understandable, should someone have the 'key' to unlocking that portion of their minds," he added.

"So what is the key?" I asked.

"You asked that already, and I gave you my honest opinion. There are exceptions, however, when God finds it necessary to unlock it for you, should you need His assistance, or should He need yours, as the case may be."

"Will I ever be able to see the future?" I wondered out loud.

He thought about it for a moment. Then a sneer pursed his lips. "Statistically speaking," he said, "if you shake a box of radio parts long enough, it will eventually become a radio. But that doesn't mean you should attempt it…"

"Touché," I said. "Now *that's* humor."

And then he got very serious.

"'Ever' is a long time," he said, and then added, "besides, I'm not sure you'd want to see the future."

35.
PURE GENIUS

"Brain researchers estimate that your unconscious database outweighs the conscious on an order exceeding ten million to one. This database is the source of your hidden, natural genius. In other words, a part of you is much smarter than you are. The wise people regularly consult that smarter part."

- Michael J. Gelb

The next day at work I kept having insights regarding yesterday's conversation. After I got home, I couldn't even wait to cross the street before I proudly announced, in JP's direction:

"So, maybe that's what a genius is: someone who uses 100% of their brain!"

He patiently waited until I had made my way across the street to acknowledge my statement. Only then, as I parked on that terribly uncomfortable folding chair, did he address it.

"Technically, it's someone who has an IQ greater than 140," he responded. "I think that number is a lot more common than people think. Apparently, Marilyn vos Savant has the highest IQ ever recorded, at 230; and she's utilizing her talents by solving puzzles in the weekly Parade column. But there are plenty of ways to be a 'genius' without necessarily having a high IQ. I would tend to define 'genius' as someone who, intellectually, can create a significant contribution to fill a void within society. Who are some people you would consider geniuses?"

"You."

He blushed, then responded: "From a religious aspect, maybe."

"Einstein, Da Vinci, and Shakespeare," I continued.

"Math, physics, art, war, transportation and literature," he answered. "There existed a void, and those people filled the void, unintentionally, in the case of Einstein and war."

"What about Hitler, Stalin, and Napoleon?" I tested him.

He thought for a moment. "Generally," he said, "the term 'genius' has a positive connotation; but in those cases, it would be hard to refute any argument that those men were geniuses."

I could tell he didn't want to dwell on that line of thinking. He moved on rapidly.

"Let me tell you about someone I think is an unsung genius; someone who filled a huge void within society. In 1960, the head of Random House Publishing, Bennett Cerf, made a wager with one of his authors, a man by the name of Theodor S. Geisel. He bet that Geisel could not write a book utilizing only fifty words. Geisel loved a challenge and went to work. He succeeded, and the book turned out to be one of the best selling books of its kind, ever.

"I got a little bored one evening and decided to count the different words in the book, because frankly, I had a little trouble believing that there were only fifty words in it myself. Most paragraphs are longer than fifty words. But it's true, here they are."

He reached in his pocket and pulled out a carefully folded slip of paper and handed it to me.

A	am	and	anywhere	Are	be	Boat	Box	Car	could
Dark	do	eat	eggs	Fox	goat	Good	Green	Ham	here
House	I	if	in	Let	like	May	Me	mouse	not
On	or	rain	Sam	Say	see	So	Thank	That	the
Them	there	they	train	Tree	try	Will	With	would	you

I looked at him in disbelief. "You keep this in your pocket?"

"It's a good conversation item. It took quite a bit of effort to sort the words out. I didn't want to just throw it away," he said. "I think it's interesting that only one of the fifty words is *not* a one syllable word. It makes for some pretty easy reading."

The words 'green' and 'ham' next to each other gave the title of the book away. "I know this book," I said. "It's Green Eggs and Ham, isn't it?"

He nodded. "I don't believe it would be too easy to write a sixty-two page book using only fifty words, but he did it."

"But isn't *genius* stretching it a bit?" I questioned.

"Not in my opinion," he answered. "I think this is an unbelievable accomplishment. It has all the right ingredients: elegant wording, vivid imagination, captivating pictures, even a moral, but most importantly, it filled a void; not quite the likes of the Theory of Relativity, mind you, but nevertheless, a void that existed in the minds of children."

He added, "And I still hold to the idea that How the Grinch Stole Christmas is one of the most inspired books of all time."

His eyes got moist and he bowed his head as though he were praying. He muttered, ever so silently, "Christmas day is in our grasp, so long as we have hands to clasp..."

For some reason, I changed a bit that night. It gave me a sense of comfort to know that a genius was writing the books my children were reading.

As I fell asleep that night, I pondered the new reverence I had found for the genius of Theodor S. Geisel, a.k.a. Dr. Seuss.

36.
THE MURDER

"I've seen things you people wouldn't believe. Attack ships on fire off the shoulder of Orion. I watched C-beams glitter in the dark near the Tanhauser Gate. All these moments will be lost in time, like tears in rain. Time to die."
  - Roy Batty (Rutger Hauer) from Blade Runner (1982).

I glanced down and saw the moonlight flicker off of the six-inch blade of the Buck knife I had been given for Christmas about ten years earlier. The night was silent. A shadowy figure of a man stood with his back to me about three feet away. In one swift move I lurched forward and drew the blade beneath his chin.

At first I thought I had missed the mark, but then he hunched over, clutching his throat. There was a muffled gasp, but it was immediately drowned out by a gurgling that reassured me that I had hit the jugular. As I glared from behind, the man fell to his knees while clutching desperately at his throat. I could see streams of liquid pulsating through his fingers, as his skin grew paler. There was so much blood. There was not supposed to be this much blood.

He rolled onto his back and looked upward as if he were in a trance. His face was nonexistent; there was just a form. His chest was heaving as he gasped his final breaths. Eventually, his fingers fell from his throat and his head cocked back against the wood of the front porch railing.

The moonlight broke through the clouds and cast a light glow over the lifeless man. I could see him now. The corners of his mouth were turned up in a contented smile.

I dropped to my knees and cradled his head as I looked deep into his eyes.

"Get up," I whispered quietly. "Please get up."

There was no movement. He was not getting up.

"Get up!" I yelled.

It was no use; he was dead. I had killed JP.

37.
THE CONFESSION

"All that we see and seem is but a dream within a dream."
- Edgar Allan Poe (1809 – 1849)

"Tell me about dreams," I demanded.

"That's not exactly my field of expertise," JP smiled. "I'm more of a visionary than a dreamer."

"But you must know something. You know everything about everything else," I said.

He must have sensed my seriousness, because he became quite serious himself. He cleared his throat and matched my mood.

"Very well," he said. "What little I know is this. Every mammal (not just humans) dreams every night, which I find quite curious. Perhaps there is a link between nursing and dreams, but the basis of that link eludes me.

"There are stages of sleep, one of which is called REM sleep, which stands for Rapid Eye Movement. It is during this stage that dreaming occurs. The pons, which is a little knob-like ball at the very top of your spinal cord, at the base of the brain, sends signals to the spinal cord, and the spinal cord, in essence, shuts down, and the body becomes temporarily paralyzed. The brain then takes over. Brain waves recorded during REM sleep are almost identical in nature to the patterns recorded during consciousness. It's almost as if the brain becomes bored, and creates its own show to entertain itself. The average person experiences REM sleep, or dreaming, every ninety minutes or so during a 'normal' night's sleep. That's really about all I can tell you."

"That's the mechanics of dreams," I said. "How about the meaning of dreams?"

He shook his head. "I'm not an interpreter. I don't know."

"Forget about what you know, tell me what you think."

He paused for a moment. This was new territory for him. He was use to speaking what he knew, not what he thought. "I think we spend a third of our lives dreaming, and no-one knows why. I think the brain is the most fascinating thing ever created and it very literally has a mind of its' own. It shouldn't be a great mystery to you that I'm a big fan of silence, and the 'A-ha' theory. There are so many instances when dreams have given people revelations in answers to problems that I can't even begin to name them all. This just supports the concept that our brain is way smarter than we know it to be. We just need to tap in to what it's trying to tell us. I think dreaming is a way of doing just that."

"So dreams have a meaning and purpose?"

"Undoubtedly, but we are so wrapped up in our own separate realities that that purpose eludes us, or even forsakes us."

"How long do they actually last?" I wondered.

"I don't know," he replied. "The only thing I've ever read that made any sense at all was that a dream lasts about as long as it takes to describe it."

I thought a minute. "I always dream in color," I said. "What does that mean?"

"It means you are one of the elite ten percent of people that do," he said. "Other than that, I don't think it means much of anything; although I would think dreams would be easier to remember if they were in color, but there's no proof of that."

It was silent for a moment as I kicked at the railing with my right foot. My face must have shown concern, because he became edgy. Finally, it was he, not I, that broke the silence.

"Are you going to tell me your dream?"

I breathed deeply, knowing I wanted to tell him the dream, but at the same time feeling somewhat ashamed. I think part of that shame stemmed from the fact that the dream made complete sense; and in revealing it, it would defeat it. There was no way, however, that I could bring myself to do such a thing.

"I dreamt I slit your throat," I unleashed.

Silence again. His face twisted a bit as he straightened in his chair. He didn't say anything. He just scratched at his abdomen and gazed off into the distance. I guess it struck me at that moment that he didn't know much more about me than I knew about him.

"What do you think?" I asked him.

"It doesn't matter what I think," he said. "What matters is what you think."

I grinned a little. "I think this is one of those revelations to problems that I would never have come up with in my conscious mind – not that you're a problem," I added.

"And what problem would that be, then?" he asked.

"The problem of whether or not you are John the Beloved," I answered. "It's quite simple, really, if you died, you are a liar. If you live, you are who you say you are."

He played along. "But you would have to make absolutely sure you killed me beyond all doubt. If you didn't do the job well enough, I'd still be alive, and it would not have solved anything; not to mention the fact that you would probably spend the rest of your life in prison. On the other hand, if I were to live, would that be enough to satisfy you, or would you always question whether or not you did the job thoroughly?"

"Whoa!" I stopped him. "I'm not entertaining the idea, I just thought it was a fascinating concept."

I continued, "When I was in high school, I had a conversation with a man over whether or not he could ever kill another human. He was a married man with a two-year-old son. He did not hesitate to tell me that if there were ever any person that he knew was going to cause harm to his wife or son, he would kill them: period. I found that hard to believe. I concluded that I would never be able to kill another man, regardless of whom I was protecting. But time has passed, and I have children of my own. I see the relevance now of his position. I know what it's like to love someone enough that you would protect them no matter what the cost; even if it means killing someone in doing so. I do know, however, that I would never be able to just out-and-out kill someone, especially you. It's not in me."

"I'm relieved to hear that," he smiled, and the tone of the conversation eased up.

"You have to admit, though, it does create a pretty fascinating dilemma."

"That it does," he agreed. "That it does."

38.
APPLYING LOGIC

"You are not thinking. You are merely being logical."
- Neils Bohr (1885 - 1962) to Albert Einstein (1879 – 1955)

That night, the gravity of the situation finally hit me. I'd been over this hundreds of times in my mind, but I'd never really thought about it. This guy claimed to have actually lived with Jesus. What did that mean to me?

I rummaged up some scrap paper and started doing what I believe psychiatrists call 'free thinking'. Arriving at my final conclusions took a substantial amount of time, but once I got there, I was somewhat amazed with what I had deduced. From a logical standpoint, it seemed flawless. From a simplicity standpoint, it seemed too easy. From a practical standpoint, it seemed like complete idiocy.

Once again, I had devised myself a truth table; one that had one assertion, one outcome, and several results arising from that outcome. I studied my scrawlings:

IF K AND L => B AND J
AND G AND E.

I neglected to mention previously that the '=>' sign designates the logical symbol for the word 'implies'. It can be substituted interchangeably with the words 'then', 'thus' or 'it can be concluded that'. In my formula, I made the following assignments:

K = I kill JP
L = JP lives
B = JP is John the Beloved
J = Jesus is who he said he was

G = There is a God
E = There is life after
death (Eternal life)

In English, what I'm proposing is this:

If I kill JP, and he doesn't
die, then JP is John the
Beloved, Jesus is who he
said he was, there is a
God, and there is life after
death.

I found it immensely ironic that by killing JP, I could concretely prove that there is life after death. The thought occurred to me that I could kill myself instead, and come to the same conclusion a little more swiftly.

I then flipped the paper over and sketched another formula:

IF K AND D => I AND P
(AND M).

Where:

K = I kill JP
D = JP dies
I = I am an idiot
P = I will spend the rest
of my life in prison
M = JP is (or used to be)
mentally unstable

Thus:

If I kill JP and JP dies,
then I am an idiot and I

will spend the rest of my
life in prison (and JP is
(or used to be) mentally
unstable).

When weighing the two possibilities, I deduced that
the letter "I's" representation was true no matter what the
outcome. Nonetheless, I found the fact that I could 'prove
God' quite an interesting notion. Men had been searching
from the beginning of time to do that, and, to my
knowledge, had failed to do so. I had found, or so it seemed
to me, something that no other man had ever discovered: an
irrefutable way to prove that there is a God. All I had to do
was break one of His commandments to do it.

Then another thought crept into my mind. Suppose
JP *was* John the Beloved, and word got out. Am I the only
psychotic in the world that could figure out what it would
mean if he really couldn't die? Aren't there hundreds,
possibly even thousands, of people in the world who would
gladly put a bullet in JP's head to prove there is, or is not, a
God?

Suddenly, JP's concept of seclusion and secrecy
meant substantially more to me than it had before. If John
the Beloved were alive today he most certainly would *not* be
in the limelight. To do so would be inviting irrational,
criminal behavior, not unlike I was exhibiting right now. Six
hundred years ago, if you hit the limelight, you could move
on and eventually be forgotten. Today, if you hit the
limelight, you're known worldwide. There would be no
place to hide. Except possibly across the street from Bryce
Anderson, in Missoula, Montana.

39.
THE CHIPS ARE DOWN

"We choose our joys and sorrows long before we experience them."
- Kahlil Gibran (1883 – 1931)

He looked different today. Instead of the usual chipper person that I had become accustomed to, he sat on the porch with his head cradled in his left hand, as if he had a severe headache. I approached slowly, because I knew something was wrong, and I wasn't sure whether or not he wanted me there at all. I concluded that if he didn't want me there, he wouldn't be on his porch at our regularly appointed meeting time.

He glanced up at me as I approached the stairs, but said nothing. Had he been crying? His eyes were red and watery. He tipped his head toward the seat next to him to indicate that I should sit down. I did. It was then that I noted that in his right hand he held a green plastic ant farm. He was focusing on it rather intently.

I said nothing. I knew whatever it was he was waiting for would be brought out in due time. I had grown quite fond of our moments of silence together, anyway, although this one was a bit unnerving.

"I'm leaving tomorrow," he whispered quietly.

My eyes bore holes in the side of his head as I awaited further explanation. To my dismay, it didn't come.

"What do you mean, leaving?" I asked.

"I mean I'm leaving. I'm moving on," he clarified.

"You just got here," I scoffed. "When you coming back?"

"I won't be coming back. I need to move on. It's time I moved on."

I had a brief moment of panic. Our last few conversations had been, well, different, and I thought maybe he was confused about my intentions. "You leaving because of me?" I wondered out loud.

"No, no, not at all. Please don't even start to think that. I just have to move on. It's time," he said.

I sat there in stunned silence for what seemed like a small slice of forever. Finally, I muttered the only words I could think of that summarized the situation: "This sucks."

"What about your house? You just got here," I prodded.

His words were slow and deliberate. "I knew I wouldn't be here that long when I moved in. I'm only renting. I've paid through January 1st. I'd appreciate it if you'd keep an eye on it for me. Here's the key – you'll need it."

I could feel myself getting angry. From the first through the eighth grade I can remember about six best friends I had had, or forced myself to have. It seemed like I had to find a new one every summer. The sole reason for that was that they had moved: they left me. Why was it that I could never pick a best friend that could stay put? My childhood trauma was coming back to haunt me.

"No. This is wrong. You can't leave yet. We're not...done," I whined. "Where are you going?"

He looked at me as if to say, 'Please don't ask again, because you know I can't answer that,' but he didn't say anything. He didn't need to. I understood.

He placed the ant farm on the porch to the right of his chair. Then he bent fully and grabbed the large wooden cup he had shown me before, the one that had housed his unusual wood chip collection. Cautiously, purposefully, he pulled the pieces out of the cup one by one, explaining them as he did.

"When I returned to Capernaum, after being released from Patmos, I was overwhelmed by the lack of tangible items I possessed. I knew nobody. The city had changed. I ached to have something that I could associate with.

"I returned to Gethsemane, where my best friend had died. It seemed only natural that I take some piece of the Garden with me."

He pulled the twig of olive from the cup and gently laid it on his knee.

He reached in the cup and pulled out the stalk of cedar.

"This is not from my Father's fleet, but it is from a fishing vessel on Galilee. I keep it to remind me of my family."

He laid the cedar next to the olive twig, and reached again into the cup.

"Gingko is known throughout Asia as a healing tree. I keep this to remind me of my early years in Asia as Prester John, a time in which I myself needed to find healing, from the pains of a lost past.

"The Baobab represents the time I spent in Africa, during the waning years of my existence as Prester John."

He paused for a moment before he drew out the next splinter of wood. I knew this would be the most painful for him, so I waited quietly.

"The palm represents the Isle of Madagascar, and, of course, Sarala. I loved those days."

Silence again, as he reflected on his past. He pulled the final piece of wood from the cup.

"And the mighty oak, splintered from the decks of the USS West Point. This piece represents my voyage to America. A free man who will never quite be free."

He carefully slipped the pieces of wood back into the cup one at a time.

"My life, in wood," he ended.

Again, it was silent for a long moment as we both struggled for something else to say. Finally, I put forth an effort to lighten the mood.

"Wherever you're going, you should swing up north through Glacier National Park before you leave Montana. If there is a God, and He ever comes to Earth, that's where He visits. There's lots of wood there, too," I added.

"Been there; and I agree. Gorgeous country. Unbelievably clear water," he said.

"You need a hand packing?" I asked, but already knew the answer.

"It takes me about ten minutes to pack," he said. "I'll be fine."

Then, the final silence set in. I don't know what he was thinking, but I recall quite vividly what I was thinking. I was wondering how I was going to form the words to tell another man that I loved him. I knew this particular man would understand, but with society being what it was, it just didn't feel right. I have enough trouble telling my wife that I love her. I copped out. I couldn't do it.

This time I was the one who spoke deliberately, "John," I said, "thank you for being you. My life has been remarkably meaningful since we met. I have quite literally lived for our half hour each day. I just can't even start to say how you've made a difference in my life. You have been a Godsend."

For the second time in the last two months, JP embraced me. This time, there was no hesitancy on my part: I embraced him back. There was no shame. There was no confusion. As we both shed tears of sorrow and friendship, I thought to myself, 'Truly, this man is Beloved'.

"I'll miss you," I managed to choke out.

"And I you," he replied.

40.
BEHIND BLUE EYES

"No single avenue of knowledge has given us the whole truth about life. No one single approach to truth can stand alone. We need them all to supplement one another and to verify one another as much as it is possible for them to do. Knowledge, which appeals to our mind, warms our hearts, is verified in experience, and is attested to by trustworthy witnesses in their respective fields, is most certainly part of the truth we seek."

- Lowell Bennion (1908 - 1996)

Two a.m. and I'm wide-awake. I could hear the effortless puffs of Gwen's breathing as she slept peacefully by my side. Even on the best of nights I can't sleep, but this was beyond that. I was amazed I'd made it 'til two. My insides felt like a blender had made its way through them; but at the same time, my mind was at ease. I would have expected otherwise.

I silently rolled from my spot on the bed and grabbed a pair of sweats from the closet. After relieving myself, I pulled them on and went to the refrigerator to chug some milk from the carton. It's amazing how quiet your own house can be when all of the occupants, particularly the smaller ones, are all sleeping soundly.

I ducked in to Valerie's room to replace the quilt on her bed that had fallen to the floor. Her red nightgown posed a sharp contrast to the paleness of her cheeks. I could hear her small puffs of breath as she lay so peacefully there on her bed. She took after her mother. There's something about sleeping children that makes life seem worthwhile. How can she sleep so soundly while the world goes on around her? I've somehow always associated that with having a clear conscience. I kissed her lightly on her forehead and whispered "Goodnight".

I wandered to the front room and looked out the window. The streetlight reflected an orangish-red hew on the pavement. My eyes followed down from the ridge of the roof of JP's house to the front porch where I had spent virtually every afternoon for the past two months. I was amazed to see the silhouette of a man against the orangey reflection of JP's front window. I quietly bolted back to my room and grabbed my glasses off of my dresser. As an afterthought, I also pocketed my Buck knife that lay next to my glasses, just in case.

It was JP. Apparently we had similar sleeping habits, at least tonight. Perfect! I thought. At least I'd get to have one final word with him before he left. I silently cracked the door so as not to awaken the family, and then tiptoed rapidly down the sidewalk and across the night-cooled street.

He seemed glad to see me. "You're up late," he said with a grin.

"I was going to say the same thing to you," I replied. "I couldn't sleep. So do you always sit out here when you can't sleep?"

"Yep. I like being outdoors. The air is better. I can think more clearly."

"How often do you have trouble sleeping?"

"Every night," he answered.

"That leaves you a lot of time for thinking," I said. Then I added, "and what is it you're thinking about tonight?"

"Eyes."

"Can you be more specific?" I joked.

He paused and collected his thoughts. "I met a lady once who told me that her five year old son was having trouble with his left eye. It was 'lazy', as she put it. I asked her if she'd taken him to see a doctor, to which she replied that she had. She didn't know it, but she told me something that I found to be quite profound. She said as recently as five years ago, medical thinking would have required placing a patch over her son's weaker left eye to 'give it the rest' it needed to heal. Today, however, medical procedure has taken to 'thinking outside of the box' and the doctor did indeed give her a patch for her son to wear – but over his right eye."

"And his weak eye was the left one?" I asked.

"It was," he confirmed. "But it's recently been proven that when you cover the weaker eye, it only makes the strong eye stronger, and the weak eye weaker. By patching the stronger eye, you are, in essence, making it weaker, while at the same time increasing the strength of the weaker eye. You remove the patch when the two eyes reach equilibrium - exactly opposite of what would have been done five years ago."

"And how is that profound?" I questioned.

"I think it's applicable to almost everything I can think of, both on an individual, and a societal basis," he responded.

"I'm not following you. Give me an example," I prodded.

"Individual or societal?" he asked.

"Individual."

He thought about it for a moment. "How well do you play the violin?" he asked.

"I don't. That's my wife's job," I replied.

"How well do you know computers?" he asked.

"They're my life," I responded. "I'd say I know them very well."

"So would you say it's fair to say that you've given up playing the violin and, simply put, utilized that time instead to develop your knowledge of computers?"

"Very roughly stated, I would say that I agree with that, yes," I answered.

'What have you compromised, consciously or unconsciously, in order to strengthen your talents? How many computers are there in your life, compared to how many violins there are in your life?"

I thought about it for a moment. The symbolism in what he was asking was immeasurable. I gave a brief shrug of my shoulders that indicated just that.

"Would you say the ratio is approximately equivalent to the number of brain cells you have chosen to develop, verses the ones you've chosen not to?" he asked.

"Ah, very profound," I mocked, while at the same time noting that what he was saying was true.

"How many Da Vinci's are there in the world who have never picked up, or even seen, a paintbrush? How many Michael Jordan's are there who gave up shooting a basketball after a couple of tries because the taller person they were playing against blocked all their shots? How many Einstein's are there who never applied themselves, because they believed the person that told them they were incompetent? How many Mother Theresa's are there who chose to walk the streets instead, because their father abused them? In what areas am I a genius that I am completely unaware of?

"The true geniuses of the world don't simply excel in one area, they are well-rounded. They don't give up after one try, or because they get discouraged, they find a way around it, or, in most cases, through it. They place their stronger points on hold until their weaknesses become their strengths. They cover the right eye."

He paused, and then added, "That's what I was thinking about tonight."

41.
THE SUICIDE SOLUTION

"Men talk of killing time while time quietly kills them."
- Dion Boucicault (1820 – 1890)

The silence was compounded by the fact that we both knew that we only had a few moments left together. He must have sensed what I was thinking, because he posed a question that got right to the heart of the matter.

"Are you okay with how things stand between us?"

I fidgeted in my cold steel chair. My eyes darted from the floor to the porch railing, and back to the floor again. I didn't want our parting conversation to be on the order that I wasn't sure whether or not he was a lunatic.

"It would just be nice to know…for certain," I finally whispered.

"Some things just take faith," he responded. "Give it time, and I think you'll come to know for certain."

He paused a moment as he gathered his thoughts. When he spoke, there was trepidation in his voice.

"I, uh, am not sure whether this will help or hurt the matter, but I have a story that I once started that I never finished. With your permission, I'd like to finish it now."

My curiosity was piqued. I sat upright and cocked my head, no longer aware of the chill night air. "By all means," I said.

"When I was in Madagascar," he began, "working in the rice fields by Sarala's side, it was the first time I had allowed myself to get emotionally attached to anyone since Jesus had died 1500 years earlier. It was definitely the first time, and in all probability the last, that I'd become romantically involved at all.

"There's a finite line, but a very significant one, between brotherly love and romantic love. She completed me. In a very real way I was not the same person after her death. I viewed every day as a perpetual continuation of the curse that I had chosen for myself; a curse that I had chosen simply because I was afraid of dying." And then he somberly added, "Peter and James were the lucky ones.

"This may sound strange, but the most important things I learned in my life, I learned during the course of my *natural* life. Everything after that was just adding icing to the cake. God knows what He's doing when He assigns our time of death.

"My pain over Sarala's death was unbearable. I couldn't stand it. I couldn't live another 1600 years and watch as those I loved passed before my eyes. It was unfair.

"I found I had three options: I could watch and wait as those I loved returned to the God who made them, I could distance myself from everyone and live a lonely life as a hermit, or, I could ask God to remove my curse from me."

His body went limp as he mustered the strength, and words, to continue.

"The Chinese have a tradition, for lack of a better term, known as Seppuku. The Japanese have a similar tradition, known as Hara-kiri. Behind this tradition is the concept that to die an honorable death is better than to live a life of shame. I had had my mortality tested twice by other men, but I had never tried to remove the curse myself. For some reason, I assumed that if I were to try, the curse would be lifted."

"You didn't..." I stammered.

He closed his eyes tightly, bowed his head in shame, and wept.

"I did," he sobbed.

He twisted his shoulders and grasped the stomach of his shirt and wadded it in his hand as he slowly started pulling it upward. After he had reached his neck, he stopped pulling.

There, beginning just above his navel, and ending a little below his sternum was a scar. It had not healed cleanly. The purplish red line was jagged, with the hair lacking from the edges for about half an inch on either side. I had seen pictures of the remnants of some bad caesarean sections, but this was far worse. There had been neither stitches nor staples to help this wound heal: time alone had healed it.

With his permission, I stood and touched it with the index finger of my right hand. Somehow, feeling it made it seem worse than it looked. I slowly sat down again.

"I can't die, but I do feel pain," he said quietly. "This hurt. I passed out for who knows how long. When I came to, the wound was healed, but the scar remained – a reminder of my immortality."

"I'm sorry," was all I could think of to say. It sounded lame.

He shifted moods a little bit. He grinned. I was grateful.

"Outside of letting you slit my throat, this is about the hardest piece of evidence that I can offer you right now that I'm telling you the truth: I am John the Beloved."

My logic came back to me. He didn't know it, but he had just told me that there was no concrete evidence he could give me, but that all evidence points to the fact that there was a man named Jesus, He was God's son, there is a God, and that there is a life after death. Did this scar prove it? I had answered my own question: not concretely.

It was then that I noticed my wife shuffling across the street in her bathrobe. She squinted a little as her eyes adjusted to the streetlights.

"I might have known you'd be over here," she said. "Just couldn't resist one last intellectual fling before you hit the road, huh? Hello, JP."

"Good evening, Mrs. Anderson."

"Do I have to come home now?" I joked.

She played along. "No, but you boys don't stay out too late."

"By the way," she added, addressing JP, "Bryce is sure going to miss you after you leave, you've been a good friend to him. Thank you."

"I assure you the feeling is mutual," he replied, and I felt all warm inside.

I slipped my hand into the pocket of my sweats and was suddenly reminded that I had brought a Buck knife with me this evening. As I looked out across the porch railing, toward our home, I was suddenly keenly aware of the saying that 'All things happen for a reason.'

JP cast a curious look in my direction as I pulled the knife from my pocket and unfolded the blade. It wasn't what I intended to do, but I had the distinct impression that if I were to bring the blade up to JP's throat, he would not have struggled against me at all. I heard Gwen protesting, but JP must have known what I was doing and gestured to her that it was okay.

Slowly, I stood and made my way to the west end of the porch and squatted down on my haunches, examining the railing. I saw what I was looking for. There, on the lower Southwestern corner of the railing, the pale paint had blistered, and exposed the raw pine beneath. I pressed the blade at a 45-degree angle into the soft corner of the wood. After I had buried it about a quarter of an inch, I swiftly rotated the blade outward, causing a splinter of wood to pop loose from the railing. I gripped the splinter between my thumb and forefinger and made a clean break, about two inches long.

I snapped the splinter in two and examined the smaller of the two pieces. Perfect. I turned and held my open palm out to JP, with the splinter resting in the middle.

"I don't feel quite worthy of the company, but if you don't mind, I'd like to add this to your collection," I said, as tears welled in my eyes.

"It would be an honor," he said, as he gently took the chip from my hand. "It will fit in nicely."

I wasn't sure we hadn't said everything there was to say, and we had already had that awkward 'goodbye' moment earlier, so I motioned for Gwen to wait for me. I extended my hand, to which I had the most memorable handshake ever. He grasped my hand and our eyes locked.

"You ever gonna make it back this way?" I asked.

"I doubt it," he responded. " But you never know."

Our hands unlocked and I looked him in the eye one last time. "If you do," I replied, "I'll be waiting."

I saw one last grin as I turned and placed my arm around Gwen's waist and we walked home together.

"Bryce?" he called after me through the stillness.

I turned to face him one last time. Gwen waited in silence by my side.

"Yes…"

"Make sure you cover the right eye."

And those were the last words that I ever heard my best friend speak.

42.
THE AUTHORITIES ARRIVE

"Heaven-bend to take my hand and lead me through the fire."
- From <u>Fallen</u> by Sarah MacLachlan (2003)

The next day I went to work, but I don't remember what I did. I must have done something, because I filled the void in my cube for upwards of eight hours. My numbness from lack of sleep was enhanced by the fact that in many ways, I felt I had been cheated. I glared at my monitor in a stupor until the hour hand finally cracked the four o' clock barrier. Those final minutes were murder. I had had enough.

The stupor must have continued on my drive home, because I don't remember anything about that, either; until I made the final right hand turn up our cul-de-sac. The adrenalin kicked in as I felt my heart leap into my throat over the sight of a Highway Patrol car parked parallel to JP's house. One officer was on his front porch at the door, another waiting with arms folded at the base of the steps gazing across the street in the direction of my house.

I pondered only briefly the idea of acting as if I had made an inadvertent turn and flipping a 'U' and killing time at Wal-Mart for an hour – only because I liked JP too much, and whatever he had done, or whatever his past had been, I wasn't sure I wanted to incriminate him in any way. I had to admit, though, he had his connections. Whatever these guys were after, he had known about it and had managed to stay one step ahead of them.

I shirked the thought and decided to pretend that two Highway Patrol officers parked across the street from my house was an everyday occurrence. To avoid eye contact, I glanced down at the seat to my right as I made the final right turn into my driveway, pausing only slightly longer than it took the automatic garage door to open. As soon as I entered the solitude of the garage, I flicked the button again and waited until the door was a good two feet from the bottom before I opened my car door to get out. I had a really bad feeling about this.

My wife, whose brow was pierced by a remarkably worried look, met me at the door. "What's going on, Bryce?" she asked.

I put my right hand on her waist and kissed her forehead gently. "I don't know. And I'm not sure I want to," I answered.

My attempt to dodge what seemed to me to be the inevitable was in vain. We heard a firm rapping of a fist four times on the front door. I winced as I shrugged at Gwen and made my way to answer it. My heart was still lodged in my throat from the sight of them parked across the street from my home. Now I actually had to talk to them.

The military-like stance they chose seemed to add to the problems with my throat. They stood there like armed soldiers protecting their ground. At least they'd taken their sunglasses off; I hate not being able to see their eyes; there's something very intimidating about that.

"Hello, sir. My name is Officer Govertsen, and this is my partner Officer Holmquist. Do you have some time we could ask you a few questions?"

"Sure," I choked out, while stepping out onto our landing and closing the door behind me. "What's going on, officer?"

Indicating to whom he was referring by an extended finger in the direction of JP's house, he asked, "Do you have any idea where your neighbor might be?"

I swallowed hard to try to pull some lubrication into my throat. It wasn't getting any better. "No," I answered honestly. "He's almost always home this time of day, but he told me he was 'moving on' last night - whatever that means."

"So you saw him last night…"

"Yes. I had trouble sleeping and about two o' clock this morning I looked out my window and he was sitting on his front porch. I went over and chatted with him for a little while."

"Did he indicate where he was 'moving on' to?"

"No, sir, he didn't. As a matter of fact, I asked him and he refused to tell me," I stated.

This was almost too easy. I didn't need to cover for JP at all; I really *didn't* know anything about him. All I had to do was tell the truth. As far as I knew, he'd never done anything illegal. I didn't have anything to worry about; except what my friend had done wrong and why two cops were after him.

"Do you happen to remember what kind of car he drove?"

"Yes, I do," I chuckled. "He drove a puke green '69 Rambler with Florida plates. It was in mint condition, too. Not a dent or scratch on it."

"What was your neighbor's name?" Officer Holmquist interjected, with a very strange look on his face.

"JP," I said slowly, with somewhat of a smirk forming on mine.

"JP what?" he responded.

I sported a full-blown smile. "Believe me officer, I went through the same thing you're going through. He told me his legal name was JP. It didn't stand for anything. It didn't have anything before or after it. It was just JP."

"Did he have any family or friends that you know of?"

"I'm pretty sure I was his best friend, and I'm certain he didn't have any family. I never even saw him speak to anyone but my wife and me. He was a very quiet man that kept to himself. Really smart guy, though," I added.

Feeling somewhat like an accomplice to a major crime, and not quite sure why, I decided it was time for me to ask some questions of my own.

"So, you gonna tell me what he did?" I asked boldly.

The look that came over his face suddenly changed from interrogator to one of complete reverence. His answer shouldn't have surprised me, but it did.

"Saved a kid's life," Officer Govertsen responded.

43.
UNVEILING THE TRUTH

I'm not afraid to die
I'm not afraid to live
And when I'm flat on my back
I hope to feel like I did.
  - From Kite by U2 (2000)

"So he didn't do anything wrong?" I asked in amazement.

"No, sir. He did nothing wrong."

"Then why are you looking for him?"

"Because he's missing. We've been trying to find him since five-thirty this morning."

I hesitated a moment as I tried to piece together the limited amount of information I had been given. There was not near enough.

"Can you just tell me what's going on?" I asked the both of them.

Holmquist looked at Govertsen and shrugged his shoulders. He gave an answer that pleased me: "Might as well, you're going to read about it in the paper tomorrow, anyway."

Officer Govertsen nodded his head in agreement and related the tale.

"About six o' clock this morning dispatch received an anonymous 911 call from a payphone in the K-Mart parking lot. The caller, male, reported an accident about a mile west of that location near where Highway 93 spans the Bitterroot River at the Buckhouse Bridge. He said an ambulance would be necessary.

"When we arrived on the scene, we saw a light blue '64 Ford pickup facing east on the westbound shoulder of Highway 93. Wedged between the pickup and the Bitterroot

River below was your friend's light green Rambler, in somewhat of a 'V' shape, due to the pickup that had impaled it.

"The driver of the pickup, a minor, had apparently fallen asleep and veered across the median into the oncoming lane. Your friend happened to be at the wrong place at the right time. The kid woulda plunged into the river had it not been for your friend.

"The kid's busted up pretty bad, and your friend here can't be found. The only thing the kid remembers is waking up just long enough to see your friend, soaked in blood, cradling his head and laying him flat on his pickup seat and covering him with a jacket. He said he heard him say, 'Go back to sleep, help will be here soon.' The next thing he remembers is waking up in the hospital."

"So where's JP?" I asked worriedly.

"That's what we can't figure out," He answered. "His car was totaled, and absolutely dripping with blood. He had to crawl out the passenger door to get out. There's no way he could have gone very far on foot, but no-one has reported giving him a lift, and he hasn't checked in to any of the local hospitals," Govertsen answered.

"Is the kid okay?" I asked.

"He'll be fine. He cracked three ribs, but didn't sustain any damage to his head or spinal column. He's gonna be sore for a while, but he'll be fine."

It got quiet as my mind raced. I had a couple more questions I wanted to ask them, but I wanted them to be in their car, about to drive away, before I did. I casually made my way to their car as we exchanged farewells. They told me to give them a call if and when I saw JP again. I assured them I would.

As Officer Holmquist started the ignition, I leaned in toward the window of their car and indicated that I had something else I wanted to ask. Govertsen rolled down the window as I casually asked, "Was he pulling a trailer?"

A quick glance between the two officers confirmed what I had already suspected, but their answer verified it completely. "No," was the short reply.

I was relieved at his answer.

"Was there anything in his car at all?" I asked.

"Just blood, glass, and upholstery."

"Hmmm. That's interesting. Thanks guys." I slapped the top of their car as I backed off and let them drive away.

I watched them pull slowly away from the curb and make a right hand turn out of our cul-de-sac before I made my way back across the street. Now that they were gone, I had one last little bit of detective work to do.

44.
FOLLOWING UP

"There is a theory which states that if ever anybody discovers exactly what the Universe is for and why it is here, it will instantly disappear and be replaced by something even more bizarre and inexplicable. There is another theory which states that this has already happened."
- Woody Allen (1935 -)

I assumed that I would never use JP's house key when I had flung it into the junk drawer next to all of the other spare keys in our house that we never use. I remembered that when he gave me the key, he had used the words 'You'll need it.' At the time, I thought that was a strange way to put it, but now I think I knew what he meant, or, at least I thought I did.

I slid the key into the deadbolt and made a counter-clockwise turn. Entering someone else's vacant home, even if you've been invited, or, in this case, been given the key, has always generated an eerie feeling that I can't quite explain. Today was no different. I'd spent over a hundred hours just five feet from this living room, but I could only remember stepping into it twice. Again I had the overwhelming feeling that I was in some way an accomplice to a major crime. The silence of his home didn't help settle my stomach any.

The first thing I saw when I walked into the living room was indeed what I had come there to see: nothing. It was empty. No couch, no poster, no ant farm. It may have been strictly psychological, but it seemed to me as if the mustiness of vacancy was already setting in.

I would have liked to call it good, but I knew that to ease my mind, I needed to make my way around all of the rooms to verify what I had come there to see. I hastened my pace toward the kitchen and did a brief check of all of the cupboards, drawers and shelves. Again, I found nothing but emptiness.

My search led me down the hall into rooms I had never been in. From the looks of them, I'm not sure that JP had been in them, either. The doors were all shut tightly, and a fine layer of dust covered the windowsill of each sequential room. There were no fresh footprints pressed into the light gray carpet in any of the rooms. For that matter, there were no vacuum marks, either. I was fairly confident these rooms had not been used at all during JP's tenure here.

The final door at the end of the hall gave me the creeps. I peered through it down an unfinished stairwell that led to an equally unfinished basement. All I could see from the top of the stairs was gray cement, ten feet below. Once again, I knew I needed to go down there to authenticate my hunch.

The stairs creaked as I sidestepped down them, as if at any moment I would want to make a hasty retreat back up them to escape the monsters that lurked in the dungeon below. I was greatly relieved when I placed my left foot on the bare cement and found myself at the eastern end of one very large, very empty, room. Transparent sheets of plastic clung to the studs along the walls, holding in vats of billowy yellow fiberglass insulation. Along the northwestern wall about twenty feet in front of me were the remnants of where someone had once begun framing, but shortly thereafter had given up. Several dead flies dotted the unframed cement windowsills. Again, a layer of fine dust covered the floor throughout, and the only footprints to be seen were the ones I had just created.

Having satisfied my curiosity, I made the aforementioned hasty retreat up the stairs and back into the front room. I paused at the front window only long enough to summarize the scene that lay just outside the window before me. In the foreground, a porch that held many fond memories of a man from whom I could never have learned too much. In the background, a home that held my family and all the experience and love that being a Father provides. Suddenly the solitude and silence of this house became a comfort, and a feeling of security swept over me. I wondered why I had ever questioned anything JP had ever told me. I breathed deeply to take it all in.

As I stepped out onto the front porch, I locked the door behind me. I knew that in all probability, I would never set foot in this house again. My mind was at ease, though, knowing that wherever John was, he had his books and his God-awful floral pattern couch with him.

I happened to glance at the porch railing where, less than twenty-four hours ago, I had splintered the wood with my knife. There, covering the splintered portion of the wood, wedged between the vertical wooden post and the railing, was a small white piece of paper not much bigger than a gum wrapper. My heart leapt as I read the message:

B,

You asked me the other day if I had ever changed the future. Since that time, I believe my answer has changed. Nothing that will alter the course of history, as we know it. Nevertheless, I just wanted to let you know.

Keep your face to the sunshine,
J.

As I sauntered down the steps and made my way across the barren driveway toward my home, I caught a glimpse of a tiny ant scurrying across the sidewalk, engaged in some activity that only he could understand. Ever so slowly, I squatted down on my haunches and decided I'd see if there was something I could learn from him.

I had some time to kill, anyway.

45.
MYSTERIES OF MY OWN

"When the solution is simple, God is answering."
- Albert Einstein (1879 - 1955)

Seventeen years ago, almost to the day, I met a man who changed my life. Not only my life, but also my way of thinking. There is scarcely a day that passes that I don't look across the street and visualize JP and myself sitting on that front porch, talking about nothing in particular; but whatever we would talk about, in it's own way, was essential.

There is a term used in today's Internet lingo that I find quite fascinating. In my dictionary, it's the fourth definition of the word, but its popularity has caught on, and it is becoming more widely used all the time.

Thread: noun. 4. a cohesive unit

I've found that more than anything else, JP taught me to think in *threads*. It's amazing how frequently I will begin studying one topic, and end up studying something seemingly unrelated, but in some way linked to the original thought. It might be something as insignificant as, say, an ant, and end up with something as unknown as, say, life after death.

I have become a firm believer in the ideology that somehow, all truth is related. We can jump in the pool in the middle, and swim to the edge, or we can slowly wade in from the side, and eventually make our way to the middle. But it's all part of the same pool, how deep we want to swim, or can swim, is up to us.

It is in this vein that I want to share with you something that I discovered the other day while researching Einstein's belief in God. I came across a most remarkable document on the Internet entitled Einstein and God, by Thomas Torrance. It contained the following paragraph:

> As Herman Weyl, Einstein's colleague at Princeton, expressed Einstein's understanding of light: 'All bodies in motion are defined relationally in terms of space and time, and space and time are defined relationally with reference to light, but light is NOT defined with reference to anything else. Light has a unique physical and metaphysical status in the universe – it is an ultimate factor, the Constant expressed as C in scientific equations. (thus Einstein's famous formula, $E = MC^2$). If light were not constant, if the movement of light varied or wobbled in any way, there would be no order, only random disorderly events, chaos. It is light that reveals the orderly nature of things.'

Now, this paragraph in and of itself is quite profound. But as I read it, I had an 'A-ha' moment. One which I so aptly attributed to my good friend JP, and one in which I have become a firm believer. The 'A-ha' was simply a recollection of a statement I must have picked up in church somewhere along the line and filed in the recesses of my brain for future reference. The 'A-ha' was this: that God is light. That's all it was: God is light. Being mathematically inclined, I envisioned the formula in my mind: God = Light. I then re-read the former paragraph, substituting all instances of the word 'light' with the word

'God'. What I had created made more sense to me than the original paragraph:

> As Herman Weyl, Einstein's colleague at Princeton, expressed Einstein's understanding of God: 'All bodies in motion are defined relationally in terms of space and time, and space and time are defined relationally with reference to God, but God is NOT defined with reference to anything else. God has a unique physical and metaphysical status in the universe – it is an ultimate factor, the Constant expressed as C in scientific equations. (thus Einstein's famous formula, $E = MC^2$). If God were not constant, if the movement of God varied or wobbled in any way, there would be no order, only random disorderly events, chaos. It is God that reveals the orderly nature of things.'

It was at this 'A-ha' moment that I truly missed my friend JP. I had really discovered something. There were thousands of questions I could come up with that I would love to pose to him, not the least of which was: 'Is it possible that Einstein included God as the constant in one of the most significant equations, if not *the* most significant equation, ever derived?' (I even noted that the 'C' was capitalized in the word 'Constant'). I also pondered the concept that when Einstein was studying light, he probably believed, or perhaps even knew, that he was studying God Himself.

Then, to complete the 'A-ha' moment, I dove into the Bible to discover where the 'God is Light' reference had originated. Shivers ran up my spine as I found the answer to be something straight out of an episode of The Twilight Zone:

1 John 1:5 This then is
the message which we
have heard of him, and
declare unto you, that
God is light, and in him is
no darkness at all.

    I stared at the name 'John'. I moved to the phrase
'God is light'. I noted that the verse ended with a remark
about God's constancy. Do I know the man who wrote this
passage? The neurons firing in my brain indicated an
alarming: "Yes, I believe I do."

46.
LIFE WITHOUT JP

"Keep your face to the sunshine and you cannot see the shadow."
- Helen Keller (1880 – 1968)

For seventeen years I've been asking myself the question, "Why me?" The ultimate answer to that question is a resounding, "I don't know."

Perhaps a better question, and one in which I can identify with more, is "Why not me?"

I keep asking myself, "How hard would it be to live your entire life in secret?" Eventually, you'd have to tell someone your secret, and you would have to have an incredible amount of trust in the 'someone' you selected to tell your secret to. There must be a great degree of comfort in knowing that someone else knows that secret. Maybe I was that someone.

My mind keeps taking me back to the time when JP told me that I was helping him, as much as he was helping me. Perhaps the mere fact that I offered him someone to talk to was enough, someone to help him pass the time while he 'tarried'. If JP was who he said he was, I feel as if I failed him. All he really wanted was for me to believe in him, and I couldn't do it. I needed proof, and there just wasn't any. There must have been some way for me to prove who he really was. But that way, to this day, has eluded me.

There is a song entitled "Forever Young" in which the question is posed: "Do you really want to live forever?" Before I met JP, I would have answered 'yes' to that question. But now, I don't know. Perhaps if I had a greater knowledge of death, and life after death, I could give a more concrete answer. But once again, the evidence is insufficient.

Perhaps if I knew for certain JP's true identity.

This much I do know: that if there is a life after death, we can only take two things with us, namely, our relationships, and our intelligence. I have the comfort of a wife, and three kids. I also have the comfort of knowing that, in all probability, I will pass before they do. I will not have to endure the pain of their passing.

For that same reason, relationships were too painful for JP. Instead of cultivating relationships, which to him were inevitable heartbreak, he chose to cultivate his intelligence, and he was very successful at doing so.

Whoever JP was, it was an honor knowing him. He enlightened me, and, more importantly, he was my friend. I miss him. I can only hope that somewhere, 600 years from now, he will somberly hold up a splinter of pine from a dilapidated old porch, look at it lovingly, and proclaim, "And this piece reminds me of my friend Bryce Anderson."